The Obliging Housemaid

DAVID EMERSON

The Obliging Housemaid

Remploy

First published 1966

This Remploy Reprint Edition 1979
Published by Remploy Limited, London

I.S.B.N. 07066-0860-7

Printed in Great Britain by
J. G. Fenn Ltd., Stoke-on-Trent
Bound by Remploy Limited
Wind Road, Ystradgynlais, Swansea, SA9 1AA

1

I

IN THE 1860's John Berridge was in business in London as a second-hand furniture dealer. People who saw him going to and fro between his shop in Tottenham Court Road and his residence in one of the quiet streets near the Royal Free Hospital in Gray's Inn Road occasionally wondered who the tall, middle-aged man might be. Women noticed his fine eyes and broad shoulders and thought him handsome.

On his way home through the wet gas-lit streets one Monday evening in December Berridge overtook Tom Sainsbury, who lived near the Berridges and attended the same Wesleyan chapel. Sainsbury, a solicitor's clerk, was an old friend. It was well known at the chapel that he was fond of giving people advice, sometimes in a jocular style but often quite seriously. This evening he had some serious advice to offer.

As they walked along together he said: 'Your lease is nearly up, isn't it?'

'Ladyday,' Berridge told him.

'Are you thinking of moving?'

'No. I am comfortable where I am.'

'It just occurred to me that you might be making a change. There is a capital house to be let in Cassilis Street.'

'Those houses in Cassilis Street are too big for us,' Berridge said.

'You could let furnished rooms,' Tom Sainsbury suggested. 'In your business you could get hold of the necessary furniture cheaply. And your wife and daughter could look after the lettings. With domestic help too, naturally. There's money in it, Berridge.'

John Berridge was not impressed. 'Why don't you take the house yourself?' he said.

'I did think of it. But my better half would have nothing to do with the scheme.'

'I'll consider it,' Berridge promised. 'Thanks for the suggestion.'

He had no intention of considering it but there was no harm in being civil.

'You would be nearer your shop,' said Tom Sainsbury.

'True. But I don't want the bother of a lodging house at my time of life. And I feel sure that Edith doesn't either.'

'It's a good house,' Tom Sainsbury said. He sounded disappointed.

If Berridge hadn't known Tom Sainsbury well he might have thought that the lawyer's clerk had an axe to grind in connection with the house in Cassilis Street. But Tom didn't grind axes. He merely enjoyed having a finger in pies.

There were four in the Berridge family—Berridge and his wife Edith, a son Stephen and a daughter Ruth.

Stephen wasn't Edith's son. Berridge's first wife had died long ago, soon after Stephen was born, and John Berridge had married Edith so as to give the baby boy a decent home. The arrangement had worked well, she had treated Stephen as her own child and they had always been fond of each other.

The children were grown up now—Stephen twenty-four, Ruth twenty. Stephen was dapper and towny. He liked to be thought a worldling, a good judge of a wine or a horse, though in his father's opinion the boy knew very little about either. Ruth was softer, a self-effacing, bookish girl.

At supper that evening he told them what Tom Sainsbury had said about the house in Cassilis Street.

Edith declined to take the notion seriously. 'Dear Mr.

Sainsbury,' she said. 'Always so full of his plans.'

Ruth was against it. 'I don't think I should like having strangers in our house. It would seem as though it wasn't home any more.'

But Stephen was disposed to favour the idea. 'Cassilis Street is a good address, Dad. Not so very far from Regent's Park. In a house as big as that, I could have my piano in a separate room.'

Stephen was employed at a fashionable music shop in New Bond Street and he knew all the latest popular songs. He was also an expert piano-tuner. Edith had taught him to play the piano when he was quite little, and he had taken to it naturally. Later on, when the time came for him to find himself a situation, he had known exactly what he wanted and where to go for it. His father had hoped the boy would join him in the furniture business, but the young fellow had refused. There was a determined streak in Stephen. He was ambitious, in spite of his man-about-town affectations. New Bond Street had given him a smooth, professional veneer that concealed the last traces of the Cockney accent of his boyhood. Only the family knew that he had a violent temper, for the temper, like the accent, was generally well under control now. And even the family did not know everything about Stephen. He lived his own life and kept a good deal of it to himself.

Edith observed that if they were really going to make a change at Ladyday it would certainly be pleasant to move somewhere nearer Regent's Park.

'With lodgers in the house,' John Berridge pointed out, 'you wouldn't have much time for Regent's Park.'

'Oh, but we should be able to afford as much domestic help as the place required, shouldn't we?'

It sounded as though she was beginning to consider the tenancy of the house in Cassilis Street as a definite possibility. Stephen's attitude had influenced her, John Berridge supposed.

The house dropped for a while from the conversation. Presently Edith slipped across to one of the windows and drew down a blind that had been forgotten.

'I don't care for people looking in,' she said. 'I like our domestic life to be quite private.'

John Berridge went on with his supper in silence. A passer-by looking in at the window was most unlikely to see anything scandalous. He himself had had his peccadilloes but Edith and Ruth, he felt sure, were as blameless as the strictest paterfamilias could wish. Stephen might have sown some wild oats, but his father thought it improbable.

After supper Stephen said: 'I do suggest, Dad, that we might very well consider this Cassilis Street idea.'

John Berridge was disagreeably conscious that a pronouncement was expected of him. Inwardly damning Tom Sainsbury and his plan, and cursing himself for having mentioned it to the family, he managed to produce a guarded opinion that left him several loopholes.

'In the first place,' he said heavily, 'I must find out whether the landlord of our present house intends to increase the rent when the lease comes to an end. Then I should have to know the rent and the terms of tenancy of the house in Cassilis Street. Finally, even if we do move, we are not obliged to go to Cassilis Street. There are other houses to be let in the district.'

It was not a dramatic decision but it was sufficient. The women seemed positively relieved. Stephen merely said: 'How soon can you find out more about the Cassilis Street house, Dad?'

'As soon as I have time,' Berridge told him curtly.

There were occasions when John Berridge almost disliked Stephen.

2

Berridge put off going to see his landlord's agent until the end of the week. The agent smiled affably. 'The rent of your house will be increased by fifteen pounds from Ladyday,' he said.

'There must be some mistake,' Berridge protested.

'Not at all, sir. Your present rent was fixed seven years ago. Times and values change, you know.'

'I shall have to think about it,' Berridge said.

'Exactly so, sir.' The agent stroked his chin. 'Now if you were considering a change to another part of London——'

'I wasn't. I must be near my business.'

'It did occur to me that we have a terrace of five new houses to be let at Brixton, Mr. Berridge. You could have a six-roomed house with every convenience, including Venetian blinds to the windows, for only twenty-five pounds a year. An extremely healthy locality.'

'Brixton is too far away for me.'

'The houses are in North Brixton. Nearer London than you might suppose. Within five minutes' walk of a twopenny omnibus fare to the City.'

Berridge thanked him and came away. He had no intention of moving to Brixton.

At home that evening he reported to the family the result of his visit to the agent.

Stephen rejected the idea. He for one would certainly not live at Brixton. Nobody with any style lived in those raw suburbs.

Edith was momentarily tempted by the newly built, up-to-date house, but she soon came down on Stephen's side, though not for the same reason.

'Whatever this man may say, I will never believe that it is as healthy to the south of the river as we are up here, near the New Road.'

Edith, who liked things to be called by the names to which she had been accustomed, always referred to Marylebone Road and Euston Road as the New Road.

'What do you think, Ruth?' she enquired of her daughter.

Ruth was against Brixton too. 'It would mean,' she said, 'that I should have to leave my babies.'

The others knew about Ruth's babies, who were not really babies at all. For the last year or two she had been teaching some of the younger girls at a school kept by a Miss Pick-nett in Albany Street.

Tom Sainsbury mentioned the Cassilis Street house again after chapel on the following Sunday morning. 'The rent sounds a lot of money but you are getting a lot for it. The place is standing empty at the moment.' He glanced cautiously around with the air of a man who has a piece of scandal to impart. 'The previous tenant was something in the theatrical line. His wife got mixed up with another man and made the mistake of leaving her husband. Probably he was as bad.'

Early next week Berridge got the key from Sainsbury and went to look at the house, taking Edith with him.

It was a big house. The size of it, when she was actually inside, frightened Edith.

'All these rooms,' she murmured, 'to be kept clean.'

'You won't have to do it yourself.'

'But really good servants don't like working in houses where rooms are let to lodgers, do they?'

'That depends on how they are treated. If you treat them like human beings, they prefer it to some grand place where they are regarded by the family as an inferior species.'

She clung to her opinion. 'They always seem to give themselves airs if they are in Lady So-and-So's service.'

'Balderdash, my dear. They like a good situation and that's the beginning and end of it. There is much to be said for being a general if you are with nice people.'

His own father had been a footman in the service of an

old dowager. When she died he had given up domestic service, set up as a second-hand furniture dealer, married and become a father, all in the space of less than two years. Being in service wasn't a bed of roses but it did mean that you could save money if you were careful. John Berridge Senior had saved all his vails and started the business with the money, the same business that his son still carried on.

When they had been all over the house, they locked the front door again and crossed the street to survey the place from the opposite pavement.

It looked harmless enough, a conventional, flat-fronted London house with area railings and several steps leading up to the front door. There were five floors, including the basement and the attics.

'Tom Sainsbury mentioned that there were two coal cellars, one beyond the other, under the pavement and the street,' Berridge said. 'I thought that there was no need for us to go down there. Especially without a light.'

Edith slipped her hand under her husband's arm and indicated that she had seen enough.

'Well, what do you think about it?' he asked her as they walked away.

'I should prefer to look at one or two other houses first, John.'

In the weeks that followed, they saw a dozen houses but there proved to be objections to all of them. It was Stephen who raised most of these objections. He seemed to have set his heart on Cassilis Street.

Eventually, at the end of January, they went back to have another look at the Cassilis Street house, and within a week Berridge had agreed to take it as from the following Ladyday.

When the thing was settled and the excitement had temporarily subsided, depression set in. It was a leap in the dark and John Berridge was not much addicted to leaps of any sort.

Edith, on the other hand, once a decision had been

reached, cheered up and began to make preparations. She was looking forward to the change, she announced. It would be so interesting to be keeping house for all kinds of people. Though she hoped that they would be quiet and well-behaved.

Edith was a large-bodied woman now, with a round, pink face and an affectedly refined manner of speaking, especially when she was talking to strangers. Berridge was fond of her, knowing that she was kind and good and, in her simple way, an agreeable domestic partner. Their home had always been a pleasant place to go back to in the evening.

Yet only a few days after agreeing to take the Cassilis Street house, he found himself slipping into a love affair with a housemaid in Brunswick Square.

3

He was in the stock-room behind his shop in Tottenham Court Road one morning when the shop-boy appeared. A young woman was in the shop, the boy said, and she had asked to see Mr. Berridge particularly.

'What does she want?' Berridge asked.

'It was about the sale of some furniture in Brunswick Square.'

As he went into the shop the young woman had her back to him. She was of more than medium height and she seemed to have a fine figure. But she was no longer a very young woman, he noticed, when she turned round and smiled at him. About thirty, he guessed.

'I'm from Mrs. Thomson in Brunswick Square,' she said. 'She has some furniture that she wishes to sell.'

'Very well. When shall I call to see it?'

'Could you call this morning?'

'I expect so.' He could look in on his way home to dinner,

he thought. 'Is there much furniture to be sold?'

'A tidy lot.'

'I'll be over at half past eleven.'

The woman smiled again. 'I'll tell Mrs. Thomson.'

He watched her until she was out of sight, wondering who and what she was. Her accent was not that of a companion, yet she seemed too well turned out for a maid. Possibly she was the lady's housekeeper. Whatever her situation might be, she was still a pretty, pleasing woman, and she must have been, ten years ago, a lovely girl, a girl with sunshine in her face.

At half past eleven he was on the steps of the house in Brunswick Square. A manservant came to the door and Berridge asked for Mrs. Thomson. Then, as the man was going away to enquire whether Mrs. Thomson was at home, the woman who had called at the shop appeared, flushed and a little breathless, as if she had been hurrying downstairs.

'All right, Joseph,' she said. 'I know all about Mr. Berridge.'

The man gave her a familiar glance and said: 'I'll leave the gentleman in your hands, Kitty.'

Berridge didn't like the apparent laxity. It sounded as if Mrs. Thomson did not keep her servants under strict control.

Mrs. Thomson proved to be an elderly lady with a tired, gentle face.

'Do sit down, Mr. Berridge,' she began. 'And don't go away, Kitty. You sit down too, Kitty. I shall want your help . . . This is Kitty Daniels, Mr. Berridge. Kitty came to me as a housemaid quite a long time ago but really she is more of a companion to me now. Aren't you, Kitty?' Without waiting for an answer, she added, quite briskly: 'Now Mr. Berridge, about this furniture. You were recommended to me. So I asked Kitty to go and see you.'

Berridge said: 'I shall be happy to inspect the furniture at your convenience, ma'am.'

'Yes, of course. Kitty will show you round. Some of it has gone already. And there are one or two things that I shall be taking with me.' She fiddled with the gold chain that she was wearing. 'Well now, Mr. Berridge, the fact is that I am leaving London and giving up my home. That is why I am selling the furniture. I am getting no younger, so I am going to live with my sister at St. Leonards. We are both widows now, you see.'

She rambled on for a while about her sister and her furniture, then she said: 'I must hand you over to Kitty now, Mr. Berridge. Having to leave Kitty behind is the one thing that troubles me about going to St. Leonards. But my sister has her own servants and she won't take any of mine into her house. I wouldn't mind so far as the others are concerned but I simply don't know what I shall do without Kitty.'

Berridge rose and followed the maid out of the room. 'Where shall we start?' he asked her.

Kitty Daniels opened a door on the other side of the landing. It was a bedroom. 'We may as well start here,' she said. She obviously knew all about the furniture, and they went quickly round the house, Berridge making notes in his pocket-book. As they entered one of the attic rooms Kitty Daniels said: 'This is my bedroom.'

There was nothing in the words themselves, hardly anything in the tone of voice or the look in her eyes. But he felt suddenly and uncomfortably conscious of her as a seductive woman.

'I suppose you would have preferred to stay with Mrs. Thomson,' he said brusquely.

'Stay with her here, yes, certainly I would that. But not go and live at St. Leonards. Now if it had been Brighton, I might have gone, if I had the chance. I love Brighton. Don't you?'

Berridge said that he liked it well enough. 'But I like London best of all.'

'Do you? So do I. No place like London, I always say. Though I am really a country girl, you know. Born and bred in Somerset. You wouldn't think it, would you? My parents died when I was thirteen and I was sent to London to live with an aunt. She soon got tired of me and I found myself in service in South Street, near Hyde Park. And I've been in service in London ever since.' She looked round the attic room sentimentally, as if it was home and she was sorry to be leaving it. 'Well, we better be moving on, Mr. Berridge, if you've seen all you want to. That Joseph will be coming up and poking his nose in, wondering what we are up to all this time. . . . There's no more furniture for sale anywhere in the house.'

She led the way down the narrow attic stairs, but on the last stair she paused, laughing up at him as though something funny had struck her.

'I suppose you often go into a lady's bedroom, don't you, Mr. Berridge? In your line of business, I mean. Almost like being a doctor, isn't it?'

He pursed his lips censoriously. She embarrassed him. 'Not at all like being a doctor, I should say,' he replied. Then, pulling out his watch, he added: 'I should like a word with Mrs. Thomson now, if you please.'

Mrs. Thomson was still fingering her slender gold chain.

'Ah, there you are, Mr. Berridge. Kitty has shown you everything, has she? Kitty is so clever and so obliging. I shall miss her very much.'

Berridge glanced at his note-book. 'Would you like me to quote a price for the whole of the contents, Mrs. Thomson?'

'That would be best, I think.'

'It did not appear to me that there was anything exceptionally valuable—the sort of silver and china, for example, on which you would probably wish to obtain an expert opinion before letting it go.'

'Oh, dear me, no! That has gone already. What remains is just ordinary comfortable furniture.'

'I have made some notes,' Berridge said, 'and I will work out a figure this afternoon. With your permission I will call again tomorrow morning and make you an offer for the contents.'

'Thank you. That will suit me very well. Kitty will see you to the door, Mr. Berridge.'

In the entrance hall he nodded to Kitty Daniels, said that he would be back again next day at eleven, and set off round the Square in the direction of Gray's Inn Road. He would be late for dinner if he didn't hurry.

Dinner, as it happened, was not quite ready when he got home. Berridge took out his pocket-book and began to consider what he would offer for Mrs. Thomson's furniture.

4

John Berridge's business provided him with a fair living. He was not in the front rank of dealers or anywhere near it, for he had neither the capital nor the knowledge to deal in great works of art. But he managed to make a steady profit.

He had seen, as he went round Mrs. Thomson's house, that others must have been there before him. Even if she had not told him so, he would have guessed that the best things had gone. He had been left with the merely useful articles. This did not offend him, however. Useful stuff was easier to sell. It was the staple of his trade.

Rain had begun to fall as he left Brunswick Square, a dismal winter rain. Ruth came in from her duties at Miss Picknett's school, the rain dripping from her umbrella and her boots splashed with mud. She put down on a table the book that she had been carrying. Ruth nearly always seemed to be carrying a book, sometimes a novel that a friend had lent her, more often a volume of poems. Today it was a novel, Berridge noticed, picking it up casually . . . *The World's Verdict* By the Author of *The Morals of Mayfair*. A lot of nonsense, no doubt. He himself rarely read anything but newspapers.

Stephen did not dine at home. So far as Berridge was aware his son patronised a chop-house near his place of business. But one could never be quite sure where Stephen was and what he was doing.

That evening after supper, he mentioned Mrs. Thomson's furniture to Edith.

'Some of it,' he said, 'may do for the Cassilis Street house.'

'You don't want to furnish rooms too handsomely for lodgers,' said Edith. 'They take no care of things.'

'If they don't use the furnishings properly,' he said, 'they will have to go.'

'But the damage will be done by then.' She seemed to be envisaging wrecked furniture and spoiled wallpaper. 'What I shall need is a reliable woman to live in and practically take charge of the lodgers' rooms.'

'I met the very woman at Mrs. Thomson's today,' he said. 'But I feel pretty certain that she wouldn't come to a lodging house, even a good-class place.'

'How much would this woman want, John?' Edith asked.

He had no notion. 'When I go to the house tomorrow, I may have a chance to speak to her again.'

'If she is a good worker and not pert and flighty, like so many of them, we might do worse, I suppose.'

'Much worse. But I don't think that she will entertain the idea for a moment. She is used to good service.'

Edith appeared to consider this. Then she said: 'When we were looking over the house, you said just the opposite. You said that servants didn't mind where they worked so long as they were treated well.'

'Did I?' It was irritating to be reminded of something that one was alleged to have said a month ago. 'Well, I can't see this particular servant in a lodging-house.'

At Brunswick Square next morning he was not received

by the manservant. Kitty Daniels herself opened the door to him with a welcoming smile.

'Good morning, Mr. Berridge. Did you get wet yesterday?'

'Not particularly.'

'I saw the rain come on, as you were going round the Square.'

As before she led him upstairs. 'You don't live over the shop, do you?'

'I live near the Royal Free Hospital. But I shall be moving at Ladyday.'

She was interested. 'Where are you going to?' she asked, as they reached the first-floor landing.

'Cassilis Street.'

'I used to have a friend in service in Cassilis Street.' She knocked at Mrs. Thomson's door. 'Mr. Berridge is here, ma'am.'

They went in. Mrs. Thomson came straight to the point.

'Well, Mr. Berridge, how much have you decided to offer me?'

He told her what he had in mind. 'I think that this would be a fair figure,' he added.

'I dare say it would. But I shall have to think about it. I will send Kitty round to your shop with a note as soon as I have come to a decision.'

'That will be quite satisfactory, ma'am.'

'When do you leave your shop at night?' Mrs. Thomson enquired.

'Usually at about half past seven.'

'I may send Kitty along this evening.'

Outside on the landing Kitty Daniels smiled at him again—the smile like sunshine that was probably the same for every man she met.

Downstairs he said bluntly: 'Have you got another place to go to?'

'Not yet. I haven't tried. Mrs. Thomson has promised to

give me six months' wages when I leave her service. I expect I shall take a room somewhere for a few weeks, until I get a new situation.'

'You won't go back to Somerset then?'

'Not likely. It was a lonely, desolate sort of village where I came from . . . No, I'm all for a bit of life.'

'Have you ever thought of being the housekeeper at a good-class lodging house?'

She gave him a wary look. 'What kind of a situation would that be?'

'I propose to let some of the rooms at this house in Cassilis Street that I am taking. I shall need somebody to look after the lodgers.'

'What about your wife? You're married, aren't you?'

'I am. But my wife doesn't feel that she can do all the work that the letting of the rooms will entail.'

'In poor health, is she?'

'No. It is just that up to the present she has never done more than keep house for a small family.'

Kitty Daniels studied her finger-nails.

'I'll think about it,' she said. 'I must say it sounds a funny arrangement. Not what I've been used to. But I'll think about it.'

5

At seven o'clock that evening the door-bell jangled at the shop. The shop-boy had gone home and Berridge was in his counting-house.

It was Kitty Daniels with Mrs. Thomson's note about the offer. He opened it, and read that his offer was accepted.

Kitty Daniels was looking about her curiously. 'Is this all the stock you have?' she asked.

'No. Most of it is at the back. Will it be satisfactory if I call on Mrs. Thomson about noon tomorrow?'

'I expect so. Mrs. Thomson hardly ever goes out in the winter.'

'Then perhaps you will be good enough to tell her that I will call upon her at noon tomorrow.'

The distant, formal tone seemed to amuse Kitty Daniels, and her eyes lit up with mockery, as though she knew that he had assumed that particular tone because he was alone on the premises with a pretty woman.

'All right,' she said. 'I'll tell Mrs. Thomson. I should like to look at the furniture that you have at the back some time or other.'

'Are you thinking of buying something?'

'I might be.'

'Why should you want furniture of your own, if I may ask?'

'That's my affair.'

'Have you thought any more about the housekeeper idea that I mentioned to you?'

'Yes, I thought about it. Should I have a sitting-room of my own?'

'I dare say. If you wanted one.'

'I should love a sitting-room of my own. That is why I was asking about the furniture. I've got some savings.'

Berridge pulled out his watch. 'You can take a look at the stock-room now, if you like, but it will be too dark to see much.'

He lit a lamp and they went along the passage to the stock-room.

She peered into the gloom. 'What a lot of furniture,' she said.

'Not as much as you would find in some places.'

'I am sure I could get what I like here.'

'Yes, I expect you would.'

'Would it cost much?'

'Not much. It would depend on what you bought.' He put

down the lamp and slipped an arm round her waist. 'You are a very pretty woman, Kitty.'

'Now, Mr. Berridge, I didn't come here for that sort of silly talk. Behave yourself, can't you? I thought you were prim and proper, straight I did, but it seems I was mistaken.'

That was how it began. Kitty Daniels was no novice at the game. If she took a fancy to a man, she would soon have him dangling after her, covetous and submissive.

Berridge pulled himself together. 'We are being foolish,' he said gruffly.

'You certainly are, Mr. Berridge. But don't include me, please.'

'Very well. You had better be getting back to Brunswick Square.'

When she had gone he returned to his counting-house and frowned over some bills. The bills were small ones, of no importance. There was no need for him to examine them at all. He merely wanted to compose his mind before he went home.

He was not a pursuer of women but several times in his life a woman had stirred him dangerously and he had had a bad time of it until the episode was over. Lately he had congratulated himself that he had reached an age at which he was not likely to be bothered in that way any more. Not for him, he had assured himself, the pitiful infatuation of a middle-aged man for a younger woman. And now Kitty Daniels had appeared in his life, a mere housemaid, somewhat past the heyday of her charms.

One thing was definite. She must not come to Cassilis Street.

Comforted by this resolve he went home. But as he asked a blessing at the beginning of supper, his eyes closed, his head bowed and his hands clasped together, he realised that he was still thinking of Kitty in the gloom of the stock-room, with his arm round her waist.

When grace was over Edith said: 'Did you see that housemaid at Brunswick Square again?'

'Yes, I have seen her today. I mentioned the situation at Cassilis Street.'

'And what did she say?'

'She said she would think about it.'

'What housemaid is this?' Stephen enquired.

'Your father,' Edith explained, 'had occasion to speak to a housemaid employed in Brunswick Square. The mistress is giving up the house, and her servants will be looking for new situations. Your father is of the opinion that the woman will be just what we need at Cassilis Street, if only she will come.'

'We shall need at least one good servant,' Stephen said. 'Mother cannot be expected to do the work of a house like that alone.'

Ruth ventured the timid comment that her work at Miss Picknett's would not give her much time to help Mother with the lodgers at Cassilis Street.

They all seemed to have an axe to grind. Edith was half afraid of the new and different sort of life that lay before her. She wanted a capable woman beside her to share the burden.

Stephen desired to allude casually, in conversation with his friends, to the existence of his housekeeper at Cassilis Street.

And Ruth was apprehensive that she might be called upon to give up Miss Picknett's and stay at home to help Edith.

It looked to Berridge as if he might soon have Kitty Daniels in the house, in spite of his prudent resolve on the subject. But there was always the chance that Kitty herself would decide not to come.

During the days that followed her saw her several times, when she brought messages to the shop from Brunswick Square.

'Are you going to take that situation I offered you?' he asked her one day.

'You must give me a bit more time. Something better might turn up.'

'If you don't make up your mind soon we shall have to look for someone else.'

'Please yourself.'

The day came when the remaining furniture was removed from Brunswick Square and Kitty was paid off.

'Have you got another place yet, Kitty?' Berridge said.

'No. I haven't bothered. The truth is I have half a mind to take on that situation of yours at Cassilis Street.'

'What are you going to do in the meanwhile?'

'Have a holiday. A friend of mine married a butcher in Southwark a few years ago. Very well indeed she did for herself. I am going to stay with her until I'm fixed up with a new place.'

'And how soon shall I know whether or not you are coming to Cassilis Street?'

'Can't say that really.'

She was exasperating. 'I will give you another week,' he told her. 'If I don't hear within a week that you are coming to Cassilis Street, I shall make other arrangements.'

She gave him one of her impudent, mocking glances. 'Very good, Mr. Berridge,' she said.

The week was nearly up when she called at the shop and informed him that she had decided to take the Cassilis Street situation. Something in her tone made him suspect that she had always intended to take it if she got the chance.

She was dressed smartly that day. 'My word,' he said, 'you are spick-and-span this morning.'

She looked down complacently at her garments, then up at his face. 'I like to dress myself up when I am on holiday,' she said. 'You don't think I did it because I was coming here, do you?'

6

When, several days later, Berridge took Kitty home to talk over the plans for Cassilis Street, Kitty made a favourable impression on Edith.

'I am sure,' Edith said afterwards, 'that she will prove to be just what we need. I could tell at once that she was most capable. And I was so pleased with her manner.'

Kitty, it was clear, had captured the citadel of Edith's good opinion without the slightest difficulty. Before long she might be running the Cassilis Street house as though she, and not Edith, were its mistress. Especially as Edith, during the last few years, had developed heart trouble—just palpitations, the doctor said, but she had to be careful.

Whether or not Kitty Daniels was to be the *de facto* mistress of the house in Cassilis Street, she did undoubtedly become Berridge's mistress during the brief period between that meeting with Edith and the removal to the new house. Kitty had time on her hands; Edith went to stay with her aunt at Windsor; and while Edith was away, Berridge took Kitty down to Brighton.

For years now, Edith had been going to Windsor quite often, sometimes only for a day but generally for the best part of a week. It was a pleasant town, she thought, and Aunt Sophy was always glad to see her. During the fortnight before the removal Aunt Sophy wrote asking Edith to come for a few days.

'Whatever shall I do, John?' Edith said. 'Aunt Sophy has been unwell and seems low-spirited. But I really cannot spare the time to go just now.'

She obviously wished to be persuaded that she could quite easily spare the time, so he replied that a change for a few days would perhaps be beneficial, before the house-moving began. He did not press the matter unduly. No plan to get Edith out of the way for a time entered his head. He merely allowed himself to be carried along by circumstances. And, of course, by the stronger will of Kitty Daniels.

After putting Edith on the train at Paddington, he returned to the shop and unexpectedly found Kitty waiting for him there. She wanted him to take her down to Brighton, she said. And she soon found out that Edith was away. For Berridge the battle was lost.

'What's to stop us being just by ourselves for a few hours?' Kitty urged. 'You could tell your son and daughter this evening that you had to attend a sale in the country near Brighton. You do go to sales at country houses, don't you?'

'Sometimes.'

'Well then, the sale is the day after tomorrow, see? You have to travel down some time tomorrow, go to the sale the day after and come back to London that same day. You won't buy anything at the sale because you find that there is nothing that you want after all.' She giggled. 'A wasted journey, eh?'

'A very pretty story. And what shall I tell my wife? Won't she think it strange that I didn't mention this journey to her before she went to Windsor?'

'Look here, I can't make up all your stories for you. You must do something for yourself. Do you want to come to Brighton with me or don't you?'

He still wasn't sure of the answer to that question. But he went. Stephen and Ruth accepted what he told them without the least apparent disbelief. They had, of course, no particular reason to suppose that he might be lying. To them he was merely a parent, a man whom they took for granted.

Berridge did not enjoy the trip. Kitty Daniels proved to be an even more compelling woman than he had supposed when he had only seen her for snatched half-hours. The amusement in her voice; the enchantment of her smile; the wantonness that she somehow made to appear innocuous, almost innocent; the touch of her lips: they were all entrancing, yet he did not enjoy himself.

He was afraid of being seen, possibly by one of the chapel people taking an early holiday. In his heart he would rather have been at work in Tottenham Court Road. He was too old, he suspected, for this sort of escapade. Or else he was not well cast for the rôle.

On the way back in the train he yawned, and she said: 'Tired?'

'Just a little.'

'You mustn't start getting old yet. You are in the prime of life, don't forget. Once you think of yourself as an old man, you will soon become one. And you mustn't do that. You are still handsome, you know. I noticed how the women at Brighton looked at you. They were envying me, I can tell you.' She sighed, as though for her part she was sorry that the trip was over. 'We had a good time, didn't we?'

He pressed her arm. 'You made me feel twenty-five again.'

It was only partially true, but it pleased her. 'Did I? Then it was good for you, it was what you needed.'

'I am not so sure.'

'Oh yes, I'm certain of it.'

By the time they reached London Kitty had convinced him that the trip to Brighton really had done him good. All the same the future frightened him. A single trip to Brighton was one thing. A mistress living in your own house was quite another.

His friend Tom Sainsbury had told him once about a case in which a client had lived for years with his wife and his mistress in the same house.

'I call that damned smart, Berridge,' Tom Sainsbury had chuckled.

They had been taking an after-chapel stroll one evening during the previous summer. Edith had been walking with Mrs. Sainsbury, Ruth with the Sainsburys' daughter, Agnes. Stephen did not go to chapel. When he attended divine service at all he went to church, which he considered better class.

'Didn't the wife know?' Berridge had said.

'Either she didn't or it suited her to look the other way. It came out when the man died and left the other woman a lot of money.'

Berridge doubted whether it was in him to be as smart as the client in Tom Sainsbury's story. He was not that kind of man.

When Edith returned he told her what he had already told Stephen and Ruth, adding that he had unaccountably forgotten all about the sale at the house near Brighton until after Edith was in the train going to Windsor. Another dealer had called at the shop and reminded him of it.

'And then after all it was a wasted journey,' he concluded. 'The prices were too high for me.'

'How disappointing!' Edith made the appropriate remarks but she did not seem very interested. She wanted to tell him about Windsor and her Aunt Sophy. 'I am glad that I went. She was so delighted to see me.'

Very soon now the removal to the house in Cassilis Street was upon them, and the Brighton trip receded into the background. The existing furniture was brought from the old house first, then Berridge took additional pieces from his stock-room as each stage in the furnishing was undertaken.

Kitty Daniels was his right-hand man in all this. She had both the physical strength and the ingenuity that the task demanded. There were no cross words or sulky looks so far as she was concerned. It might have been her own house that she was getting ready. Edith marvelled at Kitty's energy and resourcefulness; Ruth was inclined to keep out of the way; and Stephen, after treating Kitty for a day or two as a creature much lower in the social scale than himself, suddenly gave this up and appeared to be on the best of terms with her. Berridge was not altogether surprised at this development. Stephen was a young male, and Kitty had a roving eye.

It was difficult, indeed, not to feel worried about Kitty and Stephen. Berridge knew Kitty's power over a man. And he was jealous. Being jealous of your own son was damned disagreeable.

But whatever went on between Kitty and Stephen—if there was anything at all—was kept discreetly out of sight. And Berridge was certain that Kitty could be relied upon to say nothing about the Brighton episode. She might be something less than virtuous, but she was no fool.

By mid-May the house was ready for lodgers.

Everything had been done. Even coals had been got in. The summer was not far off but it might prove to be a cold summer and Berridge ordered five tons of Cannock Chase coals at twenty shillings a ton from a coal merchant at the London and North-Western Railway yard at Camden Town.

The coals were in one of the cellars now. Berridge had them shot into the nearer of the two cellars. The further cellar contained a pile of stuff left behind by the previous tenant. It was dry and inoffensive stuff—mainly floor-cloth and empty boxes it appeared to be—and Berridge decided that it could stay for the time being. He would get it cleared out when he had more time. The nearer cellar was ample for the coals of the family and the lodgers too.

The Berridges had a private parlour on the ground floor and bedrooms upstairs. Kitty asked for a sitting-room and a small bedroom on the attic floor. She was used to attics, she said, and felt at home there. Also she would be able to keep an eye on the young general, who was to have the third attic room.

During May Berridge advertised for lodgers, and the first arrived almost at once, ringing the bell in a manner that suggested that he did not propose to stand any nonsense from landladies. He was a Mr. Walker, a young man from Lancashire, in London for an indefinite time on business.

Berridge was at the shop and Edith received the young man but she handed him over to Kitty after a few minutes.

Berridge heard about it that evening from Edith.

'A most strange young man, I thought him. Trying to understand what he said made me forget what I was supposed to say myself. Fortunately Kitty was there and she had no difficulty at all.'

When Berridge met Mr. Walker he found Edith's strange young man quite commonplace. The young fellow knew nobody in London and he would obviously have liked to talk about Lancashire and power looms and mules to anyone who would listen, but nobody was interested. After he had been in the house a few days Kitty pronounced in his favour. He wasn't one to give trouble, she said.

Other lodgers came—a middle-aged spinster, a married couple, several elderly gentlemen. Most of them, like young Mr. Walker, gave no trouble. Some lodgers stayed only a few weeks, others seemed likely to make the house their home.

Kitty saw to everything connected with the lettings. After Edith's nervous encounter with Mr. Walker, it was arranged that Kitty should interview the prospective lodgers on arrival. If she approved of them and there was any accommodation to be let, she showed them the available rooms. She even collected the weekly rents.

Edith went to Windsor to see Aunt Sophy more frequently than ever and when she was away Berridge would sometimes go up to Kitty's rooms on the attic floor.

He enjoyed the dalliance but they only went to bed together on one occasion in Cassilis Street. There was no powerful urge behind their intimacy. He was getting on for fifty, and although she had swept him off his feet, it wasn't a lasting thing. The truth was that he valued her now more as a housekeeper than as a mistress. Her management of the lettings brought him an easy income. As for Kitty, it was clear that the passing fancy she had had for him was no more now than a humdrum fondness.

What did last, on Berridge's side, was a certain jealousy. He was conscious of a twinge of it whenever he saw Kitty talking to Stephen or coming out of one of the bachelor lodgers' rooms. She knew that he was jealous and she would give him one of her mocking looks as he went by. But they never had a quarrel about it.

Edith and Kitty got on perfectly. One day Kitty said to Berridge: 'Your wife is one of the best women I know.' She said it sadly, as though she regretted having injured Edith.

Berridge was embarrassed. 'Edith certainly is a very good sort of woman,' he said.

'Yes. Too good for you.'

The impertinence irritated him but he let it pass. He could not afford to fall out with Kitty.

2

I

KITTY DANIELS was not a truthful woman, and the story that she had told John Berridge about her origins was only partly correct. She had indeed been born in a Somerset village but her parents had not died, nor had she been sent to London to live with an aunt. The truth was that her mother had been a flighty girl, too fond of the men. The squire was having some decorations and repairs done at the manor house and one of the men employed was a carpenter from the nearest town. There was nothing about the carpenter to distinguish him from many other carpenters. Nothing, at any rate, that the village could discover. But Kitty's mother threw herself at him and found in consequence that a baby was coming. The carpenter denied that he was responsible. In any case he was married already. The baby, which proved to be a female, was given the name of Martha Daniels. Daniels was the mother's surname, Martha a good name for a girl who, one might predict, would work hard all her life, whether she liked it or not.

Thirteen years later the village girl became a maidservant. The squire's wife, a kindly woman, took an interest in the girl, whose prospects in the country were poor. The child was pretty. She also had engaging ways that endeared her to her betters. Finally she wasn't lazy. It was inevitable that she would go into service, and the squire's wife was aware that it was better for a young female to be in good service from the start, rather than drudge for a local farmer. She therefore arranged for Martha to go to London, to the house of an old friend who had taken her *protégées* before. And it was at this house in South Street that Martha Daniels began her career of service.

The country girl was lucky in her first mistress, a gentle spinster in the late fifties who lived in a domestic world of pincushions, needle-books and church services. It was at South Street that Martha became Kitty. A more suitable name, her mistress thought, than the puddingy Martha.

The gentle lady of South Street died after a few years and the servants were discharged. This time Kitty found her own employer and went to a grand house in which there was always a great deal of company. The master and mistress there lived a gay life and the servants took their tone from the top, so far as their circumstances permitted.

While she was at this house Kitty lost her virtue. But she did not follow her mother's example and have a baby. In the village she had learned of certain herbal and other methods of avoiding that mischance. And in service she had shared attic bedrooms with somewhat older housemaids who had enlightened her still further.

The man of her choice was the master's valet. He left soon afterwards and she never saw him again and certainly didn't grieve for him. She was not entirely promiscuous. It was exciting to play with men, but it was only very occasionally, when a man really took her fancy, that she had done more than play. And even then the feeling did not last.

John Berridge had been one of these men. He had required a great deal of encouragement, and when she had got him, he hadn't proved very lively. Stephen Berridge, she thought, was worth ten of his father. He was young, of course, several years younger than herself indeed, but that did not disqualify him as an admirer. The fact that he obviously meant to make something of his life was in his favour. He hadn't his father's tall figure, but on the other hand he was more pushing. She suspected that he had never had a woman yet, and this also was agreeably stimulating to her.

The situation was touched with danger. She did not want to have to leave Cassilis Street, which suited her very well. So she merely played with Stephen and—somewhat to her surprise—he did not press for more than she was prepared to give.

Once, when he happened to see his father coming out of her bedroom, he said afterwards: 'What the devil was Dad doing in your bedroom yesterday?'

She had her answer ready.

'Your father wanted to know whether those new people on the first floor had paid yet. He couldn't find me anywhere else so he knocked at my bedroom door. Does he have to ask you whenever he wishes to see me on business?'

'Of course he doesn't.' His tone was sulky and sceptical. 'It looked bad, that's all.'

'Looked bad, did it? Well, well, what a fuss about nothing! You didn't really think that I was behaving improperly with your father, I hope. A man of his age has got past that, let me tell you.'

'Why couldn't he have waited until you came downstairs?'

'I don't know. Ask him yourself if you are so interested.'

Until that day, so far as she could could tell, there had been no seed of doubt in Stephen's mind about his father and herself. From now on she would have to be more careful.

'You are being silly,' she told him, when the little quarrel had been made up. 'But I don't mind. I like you to be jealous sometimes because it shows that you like me. Don't be jealous of your father though. That's not at all nice and I won't have it.'

A few evenings later he took her out to dine at a place in Great Portland Street where the *table d'hôte* was half a crown and the cooking was excellent.

A friend of Stephen's from his place of business made a third member of the party for the sake of propriety. He was a young man called George Harris. Kitty thought him a trifle vulgar but he had the good sense to leave early.

When George Harris had gone Stephen said: 'Do you like this place?'

'Very much.'

'I discovered it more or less by accident,' he said with casual lordliness.

'It is quite refined, isn't it? I must say I liked refined places. I realise that I am only a housemaid, but having always been in good service I do know what's what.'

'You are not a housemaid now,' he objected.

'Yes, I am. A sort of superior housemaid. It is only because your mother isn't very strong and doesn't feel able to run the house that she lets me do as I do there. It is true that I manage the lodgers but I do a lot of the actual work too. More than you would think for. You are out all day, you see.'

'Well, Kitty, whether you are a housemaid or not, my mother thinks the world of you.'

'You're having me on. Still, she's a kind person, your stepmother. Not like some stepmothers. Nor stepfathers either for that matter.'

They strolled home together through the streets.

'You must know quite a lot about the homes of the gentry,' he said.

'Not much really, being below stairs, though you do see all sorts when you're in good service. And you hear the gossip of the servants' hall too. I was with an old dear called the Princess of Hesse Humbug or something like that once. She was always fancying that young men were falling in love with her. Then I went from her to a military cove, a general he was, I think. A fattish man with moustaches. He was a widower and we had an easy time there, but some of the young maids fought shy of being alone in a room with him, if you understand what I mean.'

They walked on in silence for a while, then he said: 'No young sprig of nobility ever wanted to marry you, I suppose?'

She laughed. 'Goodness, no. If they wanted anything of me it wasn't marriage. Some of them would have liked something else but they didn't get it.'

That night in bed she reflected ruefully that if she didn't take care she would be falling in love with Stephen Berridge. That was a thing to be avoided at all costs. because people in love were apt to do such silly things. She reckoned that her mother must have been in love with that carpenter after a fashion. Later on, when Kitty was seven years old, her mother had fallen in love again, this time with a good-looking labourer younger than herself. She had married him and had a baby by him seven months later. But he proved to be a brute, who knocked his wife about and beat the carpenter's little bastard too. It was partly because of this stepfather that the squire's kind-hearted wife had sent Kitty to London as soon as the child was old enough.

Kitty hadn't realised all this at the time. But she could understand clearly enough now that love hadn't done her mother any good and she didn't propose to fall into the trap herself.

Stephen had a passable singing voice and Kitty especially enjoyed hearing him sing popular songs, accompanying himself at the piano. This feat she found unbelievably clever.

'You ought to go on the stage,' she said.

'My voice isn't strong enough. It's all right in a room but no good in a hall or a theatre.'

'It could be trained, couldn't it?'

'There isn't enough of it to train. Still, it gives me a lot of pleasure.'

He didn't go in for classical pieces. Nor did he descend to comic songs. What he liked best, and, in her opinion, did perfectly, were sentimental songs such as Henry Smart's *Come Back to Me* and *Estelle*, that he had heard at the Monday Popular Concerts. He had the music and could read it, which to Kitty was itself something to wonder at. Sometimes he would play piano pieces with no words like the lovely waltzes of Strauss and Lanner and Labitzky. Stephen knew all the names of the popular composers. Working in a music shop, he explained, he had to know them.

Always it was the romantic pieces that he played or sang for her. His fingers would linger on the keys and his eyes, which were ordinarily too sharp for some tastes, became tender and rather sad. Marches and polkas and galops he hardly ever played.

'Not my style,' he said, with a soft look at her.

She wished now that she was still a virgin. She had never been, she hoped, the sort of tiresome woman who insists on telling people about the men in her life. And where Stephen was concerned she was determined that the past should be a closed book, so far as it was in her power to keep it closed. But there was always the risk that he might find out things about her. With his father in the house this was more than possible, though she had to admit that Mr. Berridge was not a loose talker. When he was alone with her they talked chiefly about the lodgers. Occasionally, however, he did mention Stephen.

'I am glad that you get on well with my son,' he said once.

'Why ever shouldn't I get on with him?'

'Oh, it is nothing really.'

'It must be something or you wouldn't have mentioned it.'

'Well, he used to have a violent temper. But he seems to have grown out of it.'

'He must have done. I must say I never saw any signs of bad temper in Mr. Stephen.'

He turned and looked at her in the diffident way he had when he was conscious of treading on possibly dangerous ground.

'Nothing serious between you and Stephen, is there, Kitty?'

She felt herself flushing. 'Of course there isn't anything serious,' she protested. 'What an idea! I admire him, of course, and I think he is a young man with a future before him. He's been kind to me, taking me out and playing the piano to me and everything. But if he was serious he'd be looking for someone better than a housemaid five years older than himself, wouldn't he?'

He was obviously embarrassed. 'I thought,' he said, 'that I ought to have a word with you. After what you and I have been to each other, I mean. If Stephen were to fall in love with you, it would be most unfortunate.'

'There is no question of anyone falling in love.'

He went off with a fatherly sort of smile, and she dismissed him from her mind. Several nights later Stephen took her to see Mr. and Mrs. Dion Boucicault in *The Colleen Bawn* at the New Theatre Royal in the Adelphi. Stephen had seen the great hit before but it was new to her, and she enjoyed an enchanting evening. Every minute of it, from seven o'clock when the curtain-raiser commenced, to the time when they got home and he kissed her good-night and she slipped noiselessly upstairs to her attic room—every minute was touched with magic.

They went to plays and concerts together a good deal, after that first evening. The weeks passed and she was very happy, far happier than she had anticipated when she agreed to take the situation. Things had worked out well, life was good and she did not think much about the future.

This was the state of affairs when, on a rainy Monday morning in January about ten months after Mr. Berridge had moved into the house, Miss Fairford rang the front door bell.

2

Kitty went to the door herself. An elderly, slightly stooping woman stood there struggling with her umbrella against the onslaught of the wind and the rain. A battered little doll-like figure she was, with fluffy hair dyed yellow and her eyebrows and cheeks painted. Some old retired prostitute, Kitty thought at first. But when the woman began to speak, the voice was not at all that of a street-walker. It reminded Kitty of Mrs. Thomson's voice in Brunswick Square.

'Have you by any chance a room to let?' said the doll-like creature.

'I don't think so. But come in for a few minutes. It is raining dreadfully hard.'

'That is most kind of you, most kind.' The lady came into the hall and looked about her. Her movements, Kitty noticed, were jerky, as though the old dear went by clockwork. 'This is very nice,' she murmured. Very nice and clean. But you have no room to let at present, I believe you said?'

'I don't think so, but I will make sure.'

'Thank you so much. My name is Fairford—Miss Fairford. I am lodging in Mornington Crescent now but I am not very comfortable there so I have been looking round for something else.'

'If you will take a chair, Miss Fairford, I will enquire about the room.'

Kitty never let a room until she had had a good look at the intending lodger. She felt very much inclined to send this old girl away. There was something peculiar about the woman—got up as she was at her age. She would never see sixty again but she dressed like twenty-five, and in a flashy style, to make it worse. And she was much too highly scented. On the other hand you could tell that she was a lady. Kitty began to feel sorry for poor Miss Fairford.

There was a room vacant on the second floor, she knew perfectly well. Perhaps it would be safe to let the old dear have it. Such a poor little scrap she had looked, standing there in the rain.

After an appropriate interval Kitty returned to the entrance hall.

'I find that there is a room available,' she said. 'But it is on the second floor.'

'Oh, I don't mind stairs at all. I am glad to say that I haven't yet reached the stage of being a ground-floor person.'

'Would you care to see the room?'

'Certainly I should.'

Miss Fairford got up and moved towards the staircase in her slightly mechanical way. Then abruptly she stopped.

'What is the rent of this room?' she demanded.

'Twelve shillings a week.'

'Rather a lot for the second floor perhaps. Still, I should like to see the room . . . Who is the owner of the house, by the way?'

'I don't know who owns the house. Mr. Berridge is the tenant and he lets off most of the rooms. I look after the lettings for him.'

'I see. Well, let us go up.'

She really did manage the stairs well, Kitty observed. But it wasn't as though Miss Fairford was a heavyweight. She was a tiny figure, mostly skin and bone as far as you could tell. There couldn't be much of her under those showy clothes that were so many years too young for her.

A queer fish altogether, Kitty decided. Though the voice reminded her of Mrs. Thomson's, the impression of mutton dressed like lamb was more like the old Princess of Hesse Humbug, except that the Princess had been a big woman.

In the room on the second floor Miss Fairford sat down and, as in the hall, glanced keenly about her, taking it all in. Then she got up and went over to the window.

'This room looks on to the street,' she said.

'Yes. But we don't get much traffic along here.'

'I prefer to be in the front. It is so much more interesting, I feel. Are there any brats in the house?'

'None. All quiet grown-up people. Except that Mr. Stephen plays the piano.'

'Does he play well?'

'In my opinion he does.'

'Well, I don't suppose it will worry me. This Mr. Stephen lodges here, does he?'

'No, he is Mr. Stephen Berridge—Mr. Berridge's son.'

The old bird wanted to know a devil of a lot, Kitty thought. Some people had more time to waste than others. And old ladies generally had the most. And the most curiosity too, as often as not.

'Perhaps you would like to think about it, Miss Fairford,' she suggested. 'I am busy today.'

'I am sure you are. And I have been taking up your time. But I won't take up any more of it. When can I have the room? At the end of this week?'

'If you like.'

They went downstairs. In the street the grey rain was still falling, but the wind had dropped a little. Kitty stood at the door watching the doll-like figure as it moved jerkily off under the umbrella. She couldn't help wondering whether she had been wise to let the room to the old dear. Old people could be tiresome. But so, in different ways, could younger people. It was a funny game altogether, this business of letting rooms.

She always told Mr. Berridge about any new lettings, but that day he came home feeling unwell, so she didn't bother him with Miss Fairford. Mrs. Berridge was worried about her husband and sent for the doctor, but it proved to be nothing serious. In the meanwhile Kitty told Mrs. Berridge about Miss Fairford but Mrs. Berridge only said: 'I leave all that to you, Kitty. I am sure that you would never let a room to any undesirable person. We will tell Mr. Berridge when he is quite recovered, won't we?'

As soon as Mr. Berridge was up and about again, his wife went down with her palpitations. Really, Kitty thought, it was difficult to imagine what the pair of them would have done in Cassilis Street without herself.

It was during the week after Miss Fairford moved in that Kitty descended to the main cellar to see that there was plenty of coal. It was all too easy to let the stock get low. The agent at the coal office was very business-like and a note sent up to him at the station yard at Camden Town would generally bring a supply next day if required. But in this cold weather one couldn't be absolutely sure. There was such a run on the coals at this time of year.

However there proved to be a good stock on hand in the cellar. An order could be put off for a week Nelly, the general maid-of-all-work, had instructions to report to Kitty when the coal was getting low. But Nelly was forgetful. You couldn't depend on her. It was one of Nelly's duties to take the coals from the cellar up to the family and the lodgers. She was a heavy, ill-favoured young woman, much given to gossip. Kitty was trying to train her to be quick and smart and a credit to the house but Nelly persisted in being slow, careless and rather dirty.

The lodgers all had their scuttles filled from Mr. Berridge's stock and paid extra for their coals. None of them so far had asked to have a separate stock of coals of their own.

Nelly thought that Mr. Stephen was wonderful.

'My dear girl,' Kitty told her, 'all the women think that Mr. Stephen is wonderful. But I don't know as he thinks any of the women very wonderful. He's all for himself is Mr. Stephen.'

She didn't really like talking in that nasty way about Stephen but she couldn't have people supposing that there was anything between Stephen and herself. Dull as Nelly was, she had probably already noticed a few things, and Kitty considered that a corrective would not be out of place.

Nelly changed the subject. 'I wonder Mr. Berridge doesn't have that other cellar cleared out,' she remarked.

'Shifting that stuff isn't going to be so easy. The people who were here before ought to have done it. I've told Mr. Berridge that he'll have to send a fellow along from the shop to shift it, but I suppose I'll have to speak to him again.'

One of Mr. Berridge's weaknesses was a tendency to put things off. When Kitty did speak to him again about the contents of the second cellar, he promised to have the matter attended to.

'Is the stuff in the way?' he added. 'Do you want to put anything else in there?'

She had to admit that the second cellar wasn't needed for anything at the moment. But of course it might be at some time or other.

He nodded comfortably. He would see to it, he told her. That, she suspected, was the last she would hear of the matter. It wasn't that the rubbish in the cellar was doing any harm. But it was untidy, and Kitty detested untidiness.

3

Miss Fairford was genteel. But she was also undeniably peculiar.

Young Mr. Walker was puzzled by her. The first Cassilis Street lodger was still in residence and there was no sign that he might be leaving.

'Who's the painted old woman, Kitty?' he demanded censoriously.

'I suppose you mean Miss Fairford,' Kitty replied.

'Miss Fairford, eh? Where does she come from, in Heaven's name?'

'She came here from Mornington Crescent. But she doesn't seem to have any home now.'

'Nay, I should think not. Happen nobody wanted her, coloured up and scented as she is. When she's been down the staircase it's like a bank of violets.'

Kitty regarded him severely. 'That is not true, Mr. Walker. Miss Fairford may use a little too much scent, but she is a lady. Her father was a gentleman of private means living at Bath, she told me.'

'That's nowt to go by. I still say she stinks.'

'And don't ladies use scent in Lancashire? Don't they like to smell nice up there?'

'They smell all right, lass, without that muck.'

'I'm sure I'm pleased to hear it, Mr. Walker.'

She had hoped, when he first came to the house, that living in London would make Mr. Walker more gentlemanly. But so far it appeared to have made little difference to him. Still he paid regularly and was out a good deal.

Miss Fairford took to Kitty and was for ever trying to engage her in conversation, hindering Kitty and wasting her time. But it wasn't easy to be hard-hearted. The old dear seemed to have no friends and spent hours at her window looking at the houses across the street, watching the people go in and come out and sometimes trying to catch a glimpse of their lives when the lamps in a room had been lit and, for a few minutes, the curtains had not been drawn.

It soon appeared that Miss Fairford's conversation was mostly about herself. Interested though she undoubtedly was in other people's lives, her main interest was herself, her own life. Her father, she confided to Kitty, had not always been a gentleman of independent means.

'He was in trade,' she admitted. 'It was his own choice. He was a younger son of quite a good family. But he didn't want to do any of the things that younger sons generally do.

He wanted to go into trade and make a fortune. He had some money of his own that his grandfather had left him and he bought himself a partnership in a business at Bristol. It was to do with importing and exporting goods. And he was so clever and energetic that the business grew by leaps and bounds and he was able to afford a carriage and horses. It was a grief to him that he had no son to go into the business. Three daughters he had, and he sent us all to school at Bath. Then when he felt that he had enough money to take life more easily, he retired from the business and went to live at Bath.'

She stooped to examine a splash of mud on her skirt and Kitty said: 'Did your sisters get married?'

'Yes. They both married, and left poor little me at home with my father. But my sisters are both dead now. One of them had two boys and the other a boy and a girl. The boys all went abroad and I have no idea where the girl is. None of them bothered about me.' Miss Fairford sighed and her bony fingers played with the bracelet that she was wearing. 'My father was quite a reader,' she went on, 'and he was especially fond of the works of Shakespeare. He named his three daughters after Shakespeare's heroines. The eldest was Ophelia and the middle one Miranda and I was Cordelia but I was always called Delia for short. Towards the end of his life poor Papa made some unfortunate investments, and so all I have to live on now is the rent of one property in Bath. But there is a good tenant, I am glad to say. I fancy you told me that you came from Somerset, Kitty. Did you ever go to Bath or Bristol?'

'Never, miss. I remember some girls in the village going into service at Bristol and there was one went to Bath but she came to no good, poor girl.'

Miss Fairford brightened perceptibly. 'What happened to her?'

'The husband of the lady where she was in service seemed to think he could do what he liked with the maids, and he got this girl in the family way and she was turned out, and when she went home her father wouldn't have nothing to do with her, so she got a man to take her back to Bath and nobody in the village ever heard what became of her.'

'Oh, these men, these men.' Miss Fairford sounded pleasantly shocked. 'I could tell you some stories, Kitty. There are a great many men in Bath with too much time on their hands, you know, and a good deal of that time is spent in pursuing women. I remember one man in particular, a friend of my father's. He used to come to our house frequently. Not a young man by any means. He was bald and wore spectacles. But he was a terrible one for behaving improperly with females. And he didn't stop at a little pat or a sly pinch either.'

She giggled to herself as she enjoyed the recollection of the bald gentleman's intimate attentions. Kitty was amused but also slightly disgusted. Really the old dear ought to have got beyond all that now.

But the old dear hadn't. More and more her conversation, as the days went by, seemed to be about men and the things that they got up to. Her giggle was the infallible sign that another story of life at Bath was about to be told. 'That tiresome wretch,' she would say. 'What do you think he did?' Kitty felt pretty certain that the tiresome wretches had got a good deal of encouragement. Miss Delia Fairford had needed a husband, that was certain. As for some reason or other she hadn't got herself one, she had entertained herself with any man who came along. And now she was old and no man wanted to misbehave with her.

Kitty listened when she had the time to spare. It was doing the old bird a good turn, listening to her tales.

'Were you ever in love, Kitty?' Miss Fairford asked one day.

'No, miss.'

'Now you can't expect me to believe that. A handsome woman like you. I was in love once. It was heavenly!'

'Why didn't you marry the man, if I may make so bold?'

Miss Fairford looked sad and reproachful.

'I couldn't leave poor Papa, could I?' she said.

Kitty did not reply to this enquiry. It occurred to her that Miss Fairford had probably been quite comfortable with her father, who had doubtless spoiled her. Being single had suited her better than the hazards of marriage.

One habit of Miss Fairford's was disturbing. She liked to try the doors of other people's rooms. When she found them unlocked she would have a good look round if the room was empty. If there was somebody in the room she would apologise profusely in her best Bath manner and retire.

Young Mr. Walker was one of those favoured with a visit, as he explained to Kitty afterwards.

'I was dozing in my armchair,' he said. 'I had had a reet hard day and I was tired. Summat wakened me, and there was that old trollop in the door grinning at me as though I had asked her to look in for a chat for half an hour, like. I sent her packing pretty sharp, I don't mind telling you. I shall have to keep my door locked all the time if this goes on. Eh, but she's a beauty.'

Kitty spoke to Miss Fairford about it.

'I am sure I do try to be careful, Kitty.' Miss Fairford shook her head mournfully. 'Please don't think that I would do that sort of thing on purpose. I am not at all inquisitive. It is just that I am not used to the house yet. And I have no sense of direction.'

'Well, miss, will you please try and remember which is your own room in future? It annoys the lodgers, see? They might be doing anything, not expecting to be disturbed.'

'So they might, Kitty.' Miss Fairford's eyes lit up with a salacious gleam. 'As you say, they might be doing anything.'

She went on to talk about Bath, as she generally did. 'There was a fashionable doctor that I knew, quite a great man, with carriages and horses and servants. He used to dine with us. I remember how one evening at dinner he squeezed my hand under the table. That was just the beginning. He used to like to try and get me alone. And the stories he would tell about his patients!' The schoolgirl giggle rippled out. 'He never mentioned any names. But the things he told me!'

Kitty sometimes wished that Stephen would be as daring as the Bath doctor. Stephen never overstepped the mark, which was funny in a man, especially as he obviously liked being with her.

The situation was complicated by the unexpected flaring up of Mr. Berridge's infatuation for her. Men, she knew, were subject to such attacks, and this attack proved difficult to keep off. Her old fancy for him had vanished. Besides it simply wasn't decent, when you were in love with the son, to let the father make love to you. But Mr. Berridge was the master of the house. He could get rid of her whenever he liked. It would be a silly thing for him to do, but that might not stop him doing it. And she did not want to leave Cassilis Street.

So she temporised, giving way to him up to a certain point in order to keep him quiet, but always finding some excuse for not going beyond that point.

'I suppose you've got some younger man in tow,' he complained. 'Some young fellow like Stephen.'

They were together in her sitting-room upstairs.

'I haven't got any young man,' she assured him vehemently. 'And if you don't believe me you can do the other thing.'

His doubt and discontent showed in his face. 'You're not in love with me now,' he grumbled.

'No, I'm not. And I never have been. You just took my fancy for a while and that was all.'

He looked so downcast that she had pity on him for old times' sake, and she was on his lap and lying back in his arms when the door opened and Miss Fairford put her head into the room.

4

Kitty jumped off Mr. Berridge's lap. She was very angry. 'What do you want, Miss Fairford?'

Miss Fairford's face had been a picture of lascivious delight, but Kitty's menacing manner seemed to frighten her.

'I am extremely sorry, Kitty. I just came up to pay my rent.'

'This is my private room, I would have you know. When I want your rent I will come to you and ask for it.'

'I am so sorry. I didn't mean to intrude.'

The poor old creature backed towards the head of the attic stairs and Kitty shut the door. Then she turned the fire of her wrath on to Berridge.

'Why didn't you lock the door after you when you came in?' she demanded

'I forgot. But in any case I don't consider it very wise to lock myself in with you. Somebody might come up here to speak to you, and it wouldn't look well if we were to be found locked in together.'

'Better that than to be seen like Miss Fairford found us.'

'That was just bad luck.'

'Was it? You don't know the lady as well as what I do. She probably spied you coming up and thought she would surprise us. As she did, the old hag.' Kitty's tongue clicked in vexation. 'The trouble is that she won't keep it to herself.'

Mr. Berridge merely shrugged. 'If you suspected that this might happen, why didn't you turn the key yourself?'

'Because I was a fool, I suppose. I took a chance. As a matter of fact I thought she was out. And nobody else would be likely to come poking around up here except Nelly, and she's busy in the kitchen. Miss Fairford will have to go. I shall give her notice.'

'Very well. Why not do that?'

'I don't know. In a way I like the old toad. And I'm sorry

for her, in spite of her silliness. All the same we can't have her causing trouble.'

'Don't you think that perhaps we are making too much of this, Kitty? Whatever the old woman says, who is going to believe her?'

'People generally seem to believe the bad things they hear about other people.'

The love-making was finished for that day. It could not possibly be started again after that calamitous interruption.

'You must do what you think best about giving Miss Fairford notice,' he said. 'You know the lodgers well and I hardly know them at all. And you manage them much more capably than I could.'

Soft soap, she thought, as he went out. He was weak, Mr. Berridge was. She hadn't had that idea of him when he had first come to Mrs. Thomson's. Quite the opposite, in fact. He had seemed quite a masterful man then. But she knew him better now. What puzzled her was that he didn't appear to care much whether Miss Fairford blabbed or not. Presumably he must be relying on the old dear's obvious queerness. She was mad, he would claim, or as near to it as made no odds.

Perhaps he was right about that. But one of the strangest things about Miss Fairford was that Stephen liked her. He regarded her as very good class and wouldn't hear a word against her.

When Kitty had to go to Miss Fairford's room again, she was still in the mood to give the old woman notice. She would not have entered the room if she could have avoided it. But she could not avoid it. Kitty had a sense of duty. Miss Fairford, whatever her shortcomings, was one of the lodgers and she had to receive the same attention as the rest.

The old bird was inclined to be nervous. She was afraid that Kitty was going to turn her out. The slight stoop that she always had was accentuated by her fear, but apart from that she was much as usual, mincing and affected, wearing one of her showy dresses and a pair of high-heeled shoes.

'Whatever will you think of me, Kitty?' she pleaded.

'I warned you, miss, didn't I? I told you about going into other people's rooms. I hope you've seen enough now. I hope you're satisfied.'

'I had no idea, no idea at all——'

'That's as may be, miss. People have their private lives and they're entitled to keep them private. Whatever people do is their own business, I say. Now look here. If I let you stay on—at any rate till the warmer weather—will you promise to keep your mouth shut?'

'Oh, Kitty, only let me stay. I promise you I won't say a word to a soul.' The old dear grasped at the straw feverishly. 'I have been so comfortable here. I can't tell you how truly grateful I am to you for all you have done for me.'

She began to weep, and the tears made havoc of her raddled face. Kitty gave way. It was crazy to trust a woman like Miss Fairford to keep a secret. But after all, if the old creature did talk, what difference would it make? If Mr. Berridge wasn't bothering about it, why should anyone else? Kitty decided to let matters take their course.

'You can stay if you behave yourself,' she said. 'But no more prying. If I hear of that happening again, miss, out you go.'

Miss Fairford uttered an exclamation of joy and ran forward to kiss Kitty's hand. 'You are so kind,' she said, 'so very kind. I will never forget your kindness, Kitty. Never as long as I live.'

Kitty pulled her hand gently away. The old toad was scared, right enough. As long as she stayed scared, she would probably behave herself.

'Very well, miss,' she said. 'That's all. We understand one another, I think.'

Going down to the kitchen, she persuaded herself, without entirely believing it, that the trouble had been nipped in the bud once and for all, and she told Mr. Berridge so, the next time he came up to her room and she had the chance of a word with him alone.

'If we turned her out,' he said, 'she might take her revenge by telling everyone in the house what she saw. She could be venomous, I should say. Or at any rate damned mischievous.' He chuckled to himself. 'Stephen thinks that she is most genteel,' he added, mimicking his son with more than a touch of malice.

After he had gone she let down her hair and took out her brush and comb from a drawer. Brushing her hair always had a soothing effect on her. Would she ever, she wondered, as she saw herself in the glass, become such a travesty of feminine charm as Miss Fairford? Better dead, she thought.

3

I

Stephen Berridge had never regretted the removal to Cassilis Street. In the little house off Gray's Inn Road the tone had been domestic, a shut-in sort of family atmosphere, that was good enough when one was a boy but not much fun now. At Cassilis Street one came into contact with all kinds of people. He would never, for instance, have met Miss Fairford in the old house.

Stephen would have liked to be a tall man. He was not bad-looking, he thought. His dark hair had a little wave in it and grew plentifully, with no sign of the incipient baldness that he noticed in some fellows of his own age. But he was stocky and short-legged, an inheritance, he understood, from the family of his mother, Dad's first wife.

He consoled himself with the reflection that it was often the stocky men who got on in the world. And Stephen was keen on getting on in the world. Sometimes in imagination he saw himself as the master of a fine house, in the country yet not too remote from London. How this would come about he did not know. Perhaps he would marry a rich widow. Wealthy women not infrequently came to the music establishment where he worked, and he invariably laid himself out to please and charm them. Never, so far, with any result. But one day there might be a result, and that country house would become a reality. How marvellous, on a fine morning, to walk over to the stables for a word with a favourite mare, treading the well-rolled gravel on his way with a sense of satisfaction that everything—the house, the mare, the gravel—was his own!

These equestrian dreams did not spring from a love of horses. He was, in fact, half afraid of them, though he could ride after a fashion. It was just that a man on horse-back looked more imposing than the same man on the ground. Especially if the man was inclined to be stocky.

The thing that Stephen dreaded most was to be a failure in life. He would pull any strings, however frayed they might be, if it seemed possible that they might take him a step nearer to success. One string, he had noticed, sometimes led to another. This was why he cultivated Miss Fairford. It was obvious, if only from the way she said such simple things as, 'Most kind of you, Mr. Berridge,' that she had been to an expensive school for young ladies and had lived afterwards in a more elegant world than that of the Berridges.

Stephen had persuaded his father to give him a separate room at Cassilis Street for his piano. There was a room to spare on the ground floor, and here Stephen would play—and sometimes sing—for his own pleasure or to entertain anybody who cared to listen. He had, he knew, a light touch, which was what you needed for light music. He made the tunes ripple in a way that better musicians couldn't always manage.

Miss Fairford loved to be allowed to come to what she referred to as the music-room. Stephen had never called it that himself but he was gratified. In the country house of his dreams, he promised himself that there would certainly be a music-room.

He liked to get Miss Fairford to talk about Bath. This wasn't difficult, for her conversation was in any case mostly concerned with that city. He had never been there, but he had heard about Royal Crescent, the famous Assembly Rooms and the well-bred life that was lived in and around these monuments of the Age of Taste. Bath must be the quintessence of gentility, he thought. He wasn't sure whether he wouldn't prefer it to the country house and the favourite mare.

'Why did you leave Bath?' he asked Miss Fairford one evening. 'I hope it is not a rude question, but Bath does seem to be a much more refined place than London.'

'The question is not rude at all, Mr. Berridge. I don't in the least mind questions. I think that I left Bath mainly because I had lived there too long. I had done everything too many times. I wanted a change of scene. So one morning I made up my mind to come to London. There were other reasons, of course. One of them was a man who was always pestering me to marry him. I didn't want to marry so I thought that the best thing was to run away. As I told him over and over again, if I had wished to get married I could have done so years ago.'

Stephen looked down at the piano keys. The notion of any man pursuing Miss Fairford was laughable, but Stephen was careful not to smile.

'Yes,' she continued, 'I gave up the idea of marriage because I wanted to be free. The excitement of change, new faces, different lovers—it was all absolutely necessary to me.'

He must have glanced up incredulously for she added: 'Of course, when I say lovers, I use the word in the old sense, meaning sweethearts. Nothing more than that.'

She ogled him in a way that embarrassed him for a moment. But the moment passed. There was something compelling about Miss Fairford.

One evening he took Kitty to the Imperial Music Hall in Leicester Square, where you saw dancers and vocalists and comics, and you could get a stall for a shilling. Kitty enjoyed the Imperial, and Stephen liked to be seen with such a pretty woman at a place of that sort, where the men would look her up and down covetously and envy the man who was with her. He had no intention of proposing marriage to

Kitty, however. There was no fashionable future in marriage to a housemaid.

Walking back from the Imperial that night she said, casually and as though the enquiry was merely something to fill a pause in the conversation: 'How are you getting on with Miss Fairford these days?'

'Much as usual. She comes to the music-room and chatters about Bath. The other day she asked me where I worked. I told her, New Bond Street. She said that there is a New Bond Street in Bath, and that she owns some property there.'

'She always has plenty of tales to tell about Bath. Not all to her credit, I'm sorry to say. But I've come to the conclusion that you don't have to believe everything that lady tells you. It's my belief she makes up more than half of it.'

As they passed a public house, four nondescript young fellows lounging outside and smoking cigars eyed Kitty appreciatively and made coarse remarks. Stephen ignored them but Kitty tossed her head and, when they had left the young men behind, said: 'Did you hear what they were saying?'

'Yes, I heard.'

'Why didn't you go up and punch one of them?'

'And have all the rest set on me? Not likely.'

No doubt she would have found it exciting if he had taken on those fellows but it was a lot to expect. Stephen was glad that he had been sensible and ignored them. Kitty walked on in silence for a while, then she said: 'As I was saying, you don't need to believe all Miss Fairford says, in my opinion. One peculiar thing I've noticed is that she never gets any letters, like the other lodgers. You would expect her to get one now and then from somebody, wouldn't you? And just listen to what Nelly told me. Nelly was out doing some shopping for me yesterday—I send her out on errands when I get sick of the sight of her—and she happened to meet a girl she knows that works at a house in Mornington Crescent. Well, Nelly was wasting her time gossiping with this girl, when who should go by but Miss Fairford! Miss Fairford didn't see them, Nelly says. She was looking on the pavement, and anyhow she's a bit short-sighted. When she had gone by Nelly says: "That's Miss Fairford, one of our lodgers. Did you ever see such a spectacle?" They'd both been staring after her and giggling, I suppose. Then the other girl says: "What name did you say?" And Nelly says: "Fairford. Miss Fairford". "Well," says Nelly's friend, "I know the old cockatoo as well as what you do, because she used to lodge at our place. And her name is Miss Falkland." I suppose they argued about this for long enough, and Nelly was late getting back, and that was how it all came out. So as I say, it sounds as if you don't need to take all the lady says for gospel. Even her name doesn't seem to be right.'

'Does she pay her rent?'

'Oh yes, she does that. I suppose the tenant of the property at Bath—if there really is a property at Bath—sends her his rent and she pays her own out of it. But no letter from Bath or anywhere else has ever come for her to the house, so where the man at Bath sends the money I don't know. It's all a bit mysterious if you ask me.'

The story depressed him. It sounded as if he might have been taken in by Miss Fairford, and he disliked being taken in by anybody. His vanity was hurt. Besides, he liked Miss Fairford. He couldn't believe that she was a complete sham.

He had wanted to take Kitty home in a cab but she always preferred to walk if it wasn't raining. Several times on wet nights he had been with her in a cab and had found the experience romantic and pleasurable. Another point was that she was taller than himself. This did not matter when they were close together in a cab, but out walking it was apparent to all the world. Those fellows outside the public house had made lewd remarks about the shortness of his legs by comparison with the probable length and beauty of Kitty's. He thought of the incident again now and said: 'I didn't tell you, when we were passing those low fellows, that I have a devil of a temper. So I take care to keep out of quarrels. I never know how far I might go, you see, if I lost control of myself.'

'Your father told me once that you used to have a temper when you were a boy.'

'My father told you that?' He was surprised and resentful. Dad really ought not to discuss his family with Kitty, who was, after all, a paid servant. 'How did you and my father come to be talking about me, if I may enquire?'

'Oh, bless me, I don't remember. And there's no need to get on your high horse about it either. I've never seen you in a temper myself, as far as I recollect.'

'I am sure you haven't. I never lose control of myself. When I was a boy I half-killed another boy in a quarrel. It taught me a lesson.'

He felt very fond of her that night. As they went indoors he said: 'I'll see you to the door of your room, my dear.'

She looked at him doubtfully. Their custom was to part at the foot of the stairs. But she only smiled and said: 'Very well.' The reply and the tone of voice were non-committal enough. All the same there was a caress in the smile that he did not miss.

They had reached the second floor when one of the lodgers' doors opened and somebody peered out. It was Miss Fairford, and she was full of apologies for intruding upon them.

'I heard somebody coming upstairs, and as my watch has stopped I thought that I would ask whoever it was if they would be so kind as to tell me the right time.'

Stephen told her, while she smirked from his face to Kitty's, savouring vicariously whatever pleasure it was that they had enjoyed together that evening.

'I do hope that you have both been to some delightful entertainment,' she gushed. 'I used to love the theatre when I was younger, but I have nobody to go with now, and I don't care to be out late by myself. I had a great friend at Bath, a gentleman friend. He was a surgeon—a sawbones, you know. He was devoted to the theatre and we used to go to the play together week after week. His sister used to come too for the sake of appearances but she was very tactful and looked at the stage all the time. Well, I really must not weary you young people with these tales of long ago. What time did you say it was, Mr. Berridge?'

He told her again.

'Thank you so very much. Good-night, Mr. Berridge. Good-night, Kitty.'

They went on up to the attic floor. 'That old busy-body,' Kitty grumbled. 'I've heard all about her gentleman friend before.'

'The poor lady only wanted to know the time, Kitty.'

'She knew the time as well as what you did. I expect she had been looking out of her window at the street, saw us come home and thought she would take us unawares as we were passing the door, hoping we should be kissing or something.'

'You haven't got much of an opinion of the lady, have you?'

'No, I haven't, and that's flat. I wish I'd never taken her on as a lodger here.'

Kitty unlocked the door of her sitting-room and they went in.

'I must go down now,' he said.

'Like a good boy, eh?'

'Like a good boy.'

She laughed. 'You're the boy that never loses control of himself, aren't you?'

'If a man loses control of himself, he does things that he may be sorry for afterwards.'

'Thank you for this evening,' she said. 'I did enjoy myself.'

With a tired sigh she sank into her easy chair, and he bent over her and kissed her good-night.

Then he went softly downstairs to his own room.

2

Miss Fairford put Stephen in mind of a poor old spinet, such as he occasionally came across in his work. Her day was over. But she could evoke the past, in a way that a handsome modern grand piano could not.

Although he thought a great deal about his own future, Stephen did not despise the past. Radical fellows who were always running down the past irritated him. Equality he found distasteful. There would be no point in getting on in a world where all men were equal.

Stephen enjoyed his work as a salesman in the music shop in New Bond Street, but he enjoyed his piano-tuning still more, because this took him into people's houses. There were certain customers who asked for him particularly, and one of these was a tall, gawky woman, a Miss Mitchell, who lived in Bruton Street. When he first went to the house her widowed mother was alive, but the mother had died a year ago, leaving the daughter alone in the big house except for the servants. Miss Mitchell was about Kitty's age—five years older than himself—but she had none of Kitty's charms. On the other hand she had money, which she was free to dispose of as she pleased. And as she was not a minor she could also dispose of herself. No parent or guardian had to give his consent. Charlotte Mitchell was just the sort of woman who fell an easy prey to a plausible fortune-hunter.

Stephen did not regard himself as a fortune-hunter. He really liked Miss Mitchell a good deal and had persuaded himself that he would like her as much if she hadn't a penny.

It was obvious that his company gave her pleasure, so much pleasure that he had even been invited to the house to play and sing some of the latest songs for her as a private guest. She was intensely shy and had practically no friends. Her partiality for himself was accordingly all the more interesting and valuable to him.

He decided, soon after he realised that Charlotte Mitchell was almost certainly on the brink of falling in love with him, to be perfectly open with her about himself—his parents, his sister, their home, his father's business. He even told her that his grandfather had been a footman.

Surprisingly she had replied: 'My grandfather was a butler for quite a long time but he gave it up because he had made money in other ways. He was clever at buying and selling property. And my father, his son, was clever at that kind of business too, and did it on a far larger scale. But I was his only child and I am not clever at anything.'

She had indifferent health. Sometimes it was a sick headache, at other times a troublesome cold and cough. And she suffered badly from chilblains.

Nobody at Cassilis Street knew about Miss Mitchell. She was his especial secret, and not for the world would he have boasted to his family of his friendship with the rich lady in Bruton Street. Nor did he drop the vaguest hint to Kitty.

His position was delicate. He might conceivably get the wealthy spinster to the point of marriage one day. But he was afraid of frightening her off by too precipitate tactics. Some relative or legal adviser might talk her out of the idea of marrying a penniless piano-tuner. And if that happened his chance of the country house, the favourite mare, the elegant and spacious music-room, would be gone for good. He wasn't likely to meet two Charlotte Mitchells in his life.

One evening of early spring, not long after the night when Miss Fairford had surprised him going upstairs with Kitty, he called at Bruton Street with some new songs, one of them a tuneful little thing called *The Game of Love*.

Charlotte Mitchell thought it delightful. 'I only wish that I could play and sing it as you do,' she said wistfully.

'You play very well,' he assured her.

She was pleased and looked for the moment almost pretty. His eyes rested on her face in a way that made her blush.

'Have you ever played the game of love?' he said.

It was a daring thing to say and at first she did not seem to understand. Then, as her mind took in what he meant, she laughed in a confused sort of way and shook her head.

'Never?' he pressed.

'Never.'

'Why not?'

'I don't really know. I suppose I was never that kind. Young men simply didn't come to the house. And after my father died, my mother was so low and unwell that she could hardly bear me to be out of her sight.'

Stephen was sympathetic. At the same time he could understand that men would have found it difficult to break through Charlotte Mitchell's shyness. He himself, however, had done it. There must be something about him that stirred her.

'You will get married one day,' he promised her. 'I am sure you will.'

She looked down at her lap. 'I have my mother's bridal veil upstairs,' she said. 'I got it out last week. It is really quite beautiful.'

'Brides often wear their mothers' bridal veils, don't they?'

'I believe they do. But I shouldn't want to. I should feel silly wearing a lovely thing like that.' Then, without any sort of prompting, she added: 'If I did ever marry—and I don't think it at all likely—it would have to be a man that I felt at my ease with. Someone that I could talk to as I talk to you, in a pleasant, friendly way. Most of all it would have to be someone that I felt safe with. One reads such dreadful stories of women marrying men who seemed before marriage to be all that could be desired, and then turned out afterwards to be rogues or worse. I shouldn't care about the man's social position. Within reason, of course. But I should have to feel safe with him.'

It was practically a proposal of marriage.

3

He didn't stay much longer that evening. In his heart he was half afraid of saying or doing something that might jar on Miss Mitchell, so that she would begin to doubt whether he was as safe as she had thought. So he left the house while she still felt that he was the man for her. She would probably think about him in a romantic way after he had gone, and this would tend to establish him in her affections.

'When may I call again?' he enquired, as he took his leave. 'Tomorrow?'

'Tomorrow? No, not tomorrow. I have a cousin coming to see me. He is a clerk in a government office and not very well off, poor fellow. I am afraid that he wants me to lend him money. Come the next evening, at about the usual time.'

'Shall I bring some more music?'

'As much as you can carry.'

Yes, she was certainly better-looking than when he had first met her. Women's looks did improve, he had heard, when they were in love. And with whom could she be in love, if not with himself? She had never mentioned any other man. Except her father and grandfather and this cousin, who might, for all one knew, be married already.

On the day after that momentous visit to Bruton Street, he brought home some music with the idea of playing it over on his piano, so that when he took it to Bruton Street, he would play it that much better.

Perhaps the forthcoming visit would advance matters further. It might even produce an engagement. On the other hand it might be disappointing. Charlotte might have a wretched headache. Or the cousin might have warned her against fortune-hunting young men.

It was one of the deep satisfactions in his life to retire to the music-room at Cassilis Street and play to himself.

But he was doomed to endure interruptions that evening. Dad looked in to see whether Kitty was there. He apparently wished to ask her something about some new floor-cloth for one of the rooms. Then Mother opened the door. Was Ruth there by any chance?

'Ruth does not care for light music, Mother.'

'I know, dear. I just thought that she might have popped in for a moment. By the way, Dad and I are going to Mr. and Mrs. Sainsbury's this evening. We may be a little late coming back.'

He nodded and went on playing. If Mother and Dad were to be out, there would be no more interruptions from that quarter. Ruth was not likely to bother him. Kitty might come in, but it wasn't very probable.

For a while he played on, repeating certain passages to make sure that he had them just right. He heard Mother and Dad go out, then the house was quiet.

He had just come to the end of one of the pianoforte pieces that he was practising for Charlotte when there was a tap on the door, and Miss Fairford looked in.

'I do hope that I am not *de trop,* Mr. Berridge. I heard you playing and wondered if I might come down and listen again.'

'You have sharp ears, Miss Fairford.'

'I waited outside until you had finished that piece before I knocked,' she said.

'Did you like it?'

'Indeed, yes. I liked it of all things.'

The old-fashioned phrase pleased him. 'I will play it over again. You may like it better still when you hear it from the beginning.'

His tone, he felt, was just right, just the tone that a nephew might use to a favourite aunt.

Miss Fairford was peering at the fender. 'That fender is new, isn't it?' she said.

'My father had it sent over from the shop yesterday. It is rather handsome, I think.'

She agreed. 'Those heavy metal fenders are very fine. But they have to be kept well polished.'

'Kitty will see to that. And Nelly.'

He begain to play over to her again the piece that he had been practising when she knocked. 'This is called *Moonlight on the Gondola*. It is one of H. W. Goodban's.'

She sat back in her chair and closed her eyes, the better to appreciate each delicious note. When her quick, bright eyes were shut, she looked older.

As he finished she opened her eyes again with a sigh. 'Exquisite,' she murmured. 'How splendid to have composed such a beautiful piece! And how wonderful to be able to play it as you do, Mr. Berridge! Do you think that the composer went to Venice to write it?'

'Most unlikely, I should say.'

'Oh, I am sure that he must have composed it in Venice. How else could he have got it so life-like? Did you ever go to Venice, Mr. Berridge?'

'No. As a matter of fact I have never been abroad.'

'Neither have I. Papa was always promising to take me, but it was put off year after year and in the end we didn't go at all. Well, some day I may decide to go. After all, I came from Bath to London. Why shouldn't I go from London to Venice?'

'No reason at all, if one has the money.'

'Wouldn't you like to go?'

'If I had enough money to do it in style.'

She sighed again, but this time it was not the romantic sigh with which she had saluted the close of *Moonlight on the Gondola*. It was a sigh that acknowledged the unhappy inadequacies of life.

'I love style,' she admitted, 'and one can't have style without money.'

'Kitty has a certain style,' he said, 'and she can't have much money.'

Miss Fairford shrugged coldly. 'I am free to confess that Kitty dresses quite well when she goes out for the evening.' And then surprisingly she added: 'But I should not have too much to do with Kitty if I were you.'

'Why ever not, Miss Fairford?'

'Because she is a loose woman.'

'I find that hard to believe.'

His manner, he hoped, was no more than mildly interested. But he could not conceal from himself that his heart had leapt to Kitty's defence. What right had anyone to call Kitty loose? He had never found her so, and he had had ample opportunities.

'Kitty is a handsome creature,' said Miss Fairford darkly

'True.'

'You are half in love with her, aren't you?'

She was leaning forward in the chair now, her glittering eyes fixed on him almost menacingly. The grin on her lips was sardonic and dirty.

'I would rather not discuss Kitty,' he replied stiffly.

'But I think that you should, Mr. Berridge, before you go too far. Did you know, for example, that she is your father's mistress?'

He stared at her.

'You don't believe me,' she pursued. 'But I tell you that it is true. You are falling in love with your father's mistress. I was suspicious for some time, and one day last month I found him in her room. What I saw left no doubt in my mind that she was his mistress, no doubt at all.'

She proceeded to describe, in some detail and with evident relish, what it was that she had seen.

He sat bolt upright on the piano-stool, horrified, while Miss Fairford went vehemently on and on without a pause, as though her life depended on it. And gradually what she was saying made its impression. He remembered his quarrel with Kitty after he had seen Dad coming out of her room. Kitty had told him not to be so silly. But if there had been anything between Dad and Kitty, she wasn't likely to admit it. He had been a simpleton, it seemed. Unless of course Miss Fairford was making it all up. Kitty, after all, had warned him against the old woman's tongue.

With an effort he took a firm hold on his mind. The whole thing must be a ridiculous fabrication. Yet the seed of doubt remained.

Getting up from the music stool he began to put his music away. This nonsense of the poor old lady's had gone on long enough.

'I don't wish to hear any more, Miss Fairford.'

'Don't you believe me?'

'No. I don't.'

'Then ask Kitty. No, don't do that. She wouldn't tell you the truth. Ask your father. He probably isn't such a good liar. No use talking to that scheming trollop about it. She would soon win you over. She knows how to bamboozle men, the hussy.' With a quick, jerky movement she was on her feet and her bony hands were clawing at his shoulders. 'Have nothing more to do with her, I beg of you,' she pleaded. 'You are too good for her. Don't throw yourself away on that sort of woman. Listen, Stephen, listen to me. I have money, quite a lot of money. I don't tell people, but it is true. I have enough money for both of us. Come abroad with me, Stephen. Let us leave this country and find somewhere abroad where we can live together. I will pay for everything. You don't need to think about the expense at all——'

The raddled face was close to his, the skinny body was pressed against him, the scent that she used made him feel sick. Suddenly he lost his temper.

'Get away,' he shouted. 'Get away, you old bitch! And if you aren't out of the house tomorrow you'll find your bags on the pavement!'

He pushed her violently off. That was all he intended to do. But she caught her high heel in a rug, tottered backwards, lost her balance and fell against the steel fender, hitting the back of her head on it as she crashed down.

He expected her to sit up, protesting, weeping perhaps. But she didn't. She lay still, with a look of bewildered self-pity on her face.

4

He bent over her.

'Miss Fairford,' he muttered foolishly, 'are you all right? What is the matter?'

There was no reply. Miss Fairford lay as she had fallen. He decided to summon Kitty, who was always a tower of strength in a crisis.

As he left the music-room he locked the door. Nobody must go in and find Miss Fairford. He couldn't trust anyone but Kitty to help him and keep quiet about it.

Upstairs he knocked nervously at the door of her sitting-room. She was in her arm-chair, that chair in which, according to Miss Fairford, she had been sitting with Dad in circumstances that left no doubt as to their relationship. But he couldn't worry about that now.

'Kitty,' he said, 'will you come down to the music-room please?'

'What's the matter?'

'It's Miss Fairford. I think she's fainted.'

'All right. I'll come.'

They went quickly down to the ground floor together.

'What's the door locked for?' Kitty demanded, when they reached the music-room and he took out his keys.

He did not answer. Turning the key in the lock he opened the door. Kitty followed him in and he locked the door again behind them.

Against the fender the bedizened old figure still lay motionless. Kitty went down on her knees and moved the head slightly, putting one hand under the sparse, dyed ringlets. Then she withdrew her hand and sat back on her haunches. Raising the hand for Stephen to see she said: 'She hasn't fainted. Looks to me she's dead.'

Kitty's hand was dark and sticky. 'She can't be dead,' he blustered. 'Don't talk such nonsense.'

'Very well. Better send for a doctor, I suppose. He'll soon tell you whether she's dead or not.'

'No, don't do that. Not yet, I mean.'

'If it's to be any good, now is the time to do it.' Kitty bent over Miss Fairford again, felt her pulse and undid her bodice. 'I reckon she's dead. There was a girl fell downstairs in one house where I was. She was just like this. Never breathed or spoke again, she didn't.' She frowned up at his face. 'You do look white,' she said. 'And you're trembling. Let me get you some brandy.'

'No, I don't need anything.'

'How did this happen?'

'She said that you were my father's mistress. And she wanted me to go abroad with her and live together on her money. I lost my temper and pushed her away and she fell backwards.'

Kitty didn't flinch. Her eyes left his face and rested on the painted cheeks of Miss Delia Fairford.

'The old devil,' she remarked calmly. 'And I half liked the old toad.'

'So did I. In a way. Kitty, what are we going to do?'

'We? I should say it was a case of what are you going to do. There will have to be an inquest. I suppose you know that. And if it was me on the coroner's jury I should think it looked like manslaughter. I forget how many years you get for that.'

He felt weak and dizzy. Sinking back on to the music stool he put his head in his hands.

'Oh, my God! What can I do?'

If this affair came out, as it would presumably have to, it would be the end of his plans for marrying Charlotte Mitchell. She would get to hear about it, in one way or another, even if he escaped a prison sentence. She would suppose that she had been mistaken in him. A man who could attack a poor old woman so brutally was no husband for her.

Kitty, when at last he looked up, was watching him curiously.

'Did you believe what she said about your father and me?' she asked.

'No.' At all costs, something told him, he must have Kitty on his side. What did it matter now that she might have been Dad's mistress? 'Of course I didn't believe it.'

Kitty seemed satisfied. 'It was a pack of lies. I told you what the old bird was like, didn't I? I warned you against her.'

He nodded gloomily. Tomorrow evening he would have been going to see Charlotte Mitchell again. Would he still go? Was there any point in going now?

'Cheer up, Stephen.' Kitty was incredibly composed, as though she had been used to handling situations of this sort for years. 'To begin with, are you going to send for a doctor or not?'

'What else is there to do?'

'Nothing, if you want to keep on the right side of the law.'

'And if I take a chance, what then?'

'You will have to get rid of the body, of course.'

A gleam of hope lit up his mind. Kitty was going to help him. She had her own axe to grind, but she would help him. If she got him out of this, he would be expected to marry her. Out of gratitude. Or to keep her quiet. Marrying Kitty would be the end of his ambitions. But it was better than prison.

'I'll take a chance,' he said. 'What do we do next?'

'Haven't you got any ideas yourself? Why do I have to tell you what to do?'

He didn't try to answer her. Going over to where Kitty still crouched beside the silent figure on the rug he put an arm around her shoulders.

'You will help me, won't you?' he pleaded. 'I'll do anything if only you get me out of this.'

She smiled ruefully, as though she despised him but couldn't help loving him.

'I'll help you,' she said. 'I'm a damned fool to do it, and if I don't look out I'll end up with my neck in a noose. But I'll do what I can. Now, listen to me. You know that little room on the first floor where the new floor-cloth has just been laid?'

'The room that Mr. Parker used to have?'

'That's the room. It's empty now and the old floor-cloth is in one corner tied up in roll with a cord round it. Bring it down here. It'll be heavy but you'll manage. And for God's sake look sharp. We may not have much time.'

He did as he was told. The house was still quiet. The old floor-cloth was tidily rolled up and proved to be not too heavy for him to carry. So far as he could tell, nobody saw him or heard him.

In the music-room Kitty had partly undressed Miss Fairford. Stephen winced and averted his gaze.

'Come on now,' Kitty scolded him. 'No good having fine feelings in this kind of job. You should have thought of all this before you lost your temper with her. Loosen that cord and unroll the floor-cloth. And give me some of the cord. Have you got a knife? Right then, cut about a yard off one end. There's plenty to spare.'

He cut off the length of cord and handed it to her. Then he nearly vomited as Kitty tied the cord around Miss Fairford's neck and pulled it tight with her strong hands.

'She's dead as a doornail already,' Kitty remarked. 'But you can't be too sure. Now, hold the floor-cloth open while I drag her on to it . . . That's the ticket, that's fine.'

She surveyed her handiwork complacently, as though she

had been engaged in some creditable piece of work.

'Now we must roll the floor-cloth all round her. As firmly as we can. We don't want her to slip out at one end. There, that's capital.'

They tied the remaining piece of cord round the old floor-cloth that was to be the last resting-place of poor Miss Fairford. Kitty's sang-froid showed no signs of weakening. For the first time he realised to the full that, bewitching though she was, there was a gulf between them. He and Kitty Daniels thought on different levels, spoke a different language. They simply hadn't the same standards. Except where his music was concerned, he had regarded himself as a tough and insensitive person. Now he saw that, by comparison with Kitty, he was delicately fastidious. Left to himself he couldn't possibly have done what she had done this evening.

She turned for a moment to look at a dark stain on the rug beside the fender, and as she stood there with her back to him, Stephen could see that she was thickening. In ten years she would be a big, formidable woman.

'I'll soon clear that up,' she said, half to herself. Turning back to the floor-cloth with its hidden, pitiful burden, she added: 'Stay here for a few minutes. I must get those clothes out of the way. I'll just run upstairs with them and then go down to the kitchen to make sure the coast is clear.'

She slipped out and he sank wearily down on the piano-stool again. Presumably she was taking Miss Fairford's clothes to her own room. What she meant about the kitchen he didn't understand. Sitting there alone beside his piano he wished that his father had never moved to Cassilis Street. If they had all stayed in the little house off Gray's Inn Road his relationship with Charlotte Mitchell would have been no worse than it was now. Far better indeed. Had he remained in the old house, he would never have met Kitty Daniels or Miss Fairford. And he wouldn't, at this moment, have been engaged in the terrible business of concealing a violent death in which he, through the most dreadful luck in the world, was dangerously involved.

The door opened and he started, wondering what he would say if it was Mother or Dad, just back from the Sainsburys' house. But it was Kitty again. She was looking as if butter wouldn't melt in her mouth. If you didn't know the truth, you might have suposed that she had just come in from a bible class. 'All ready,' she said. 'You take that end, I'll take this.'

They lifted the floor-cloth. It was much heavier with Miss Fairford inside. He would never have believed that her skinny little body could weigh so much.

'If anyone sees us,' Kitty instructed him, 'you are just helping me to take this downstairs.' She giggled. 'In a way it's true, isn't it?'

They went out into the entrance hall and down the back stairs to the kitchen. The door from the kitchen to the area stood ajar. On the other side of the area was the door to the two cellars. Stephen had hardly ever been to the cellars before. The nearer one, he knew, held the coals. He was just able to glimpse the black masses as they went through. In the further cellar a candle was burning, doubtless placed there by Kitty a few minutes ago. By its light he could make out a pile of boxes, some discarded furniture and a couple of rolls of decaying floor-cloth.

'All left by the previous tenant,' Kitty said. 'Your father has been going to have it cleared ever since we came here, but he has never found the time, poor man . . . Now, lay her down here with the other floor-cloth. And put one or two things on top. Not much, because we shall have to get her away before long.'

Kitty thought of everything. Hateful though he found the ruthless side of her that he was seeing tonight, he could not withhold a tribute of admiration.

'You ought to have been a man,' he said. 'A soldier or a policeman perhaps. Or an explorer. The sort of man who can cope with any emergency.'

She flung her arms around him, there in the dim cellar, beside the pile of rubbish and the body of Miss Fairford.

'I'm not a man,' she murmured, close to his ear. 'I'm a woman—your woman. You don't think I'd have done all this for any other man, do you?' Then she giggled again, a trifle hysterically. 'And don't for God's sake talk about policemen. It'll be a long time before I can look a policeman in the eye again.'

In the coal-cellar she blew out the candle and they went back to the music-room. It seemed to Stephen that they had hardly got inside the room when he heard the key in the front door.

'Start playing something,' Kitty whispered, pushing him towards the piano.

He began to play the first tune that came into his head. It happened to be a Christy Minstrel melody that Mother was fond of. Presently Mother looked in, a friendly smile on her simple face. 'Such a sweet tune,' she said. Then turning to Kitty she added: 'You look tired, my dear. Better get to bed. And you are looking pale, Stephen. I think that perhaps you have both had enough for one day.'

She went out with a kind good-night. Only then did Stephen notice that, before Mother looked into the room, Kitty had moved her position so that her skirts covered the stain on the rug.

'Your mother wasn't far out,' Kitty said. 'I've had enough all right. I'm fit to drop.' She sounded as though, now that the excitement was over for the moment, she was sick of the whole thing. 'And there's a lot still to do,' she added. 'A devil of a lot.'

Bending over him she kissed him possessively.

'Until tomorrow,' she said. 'We must have a talk about it tomorrow evening.'

He took his courage in both hands.

'I am sorry, Kitty. I shall be out tomorrow evening. I promised to go out with George Harris, the fellow we dined with in Great Portland Street.'

She frowned at him suspiciously. 'Going out enjoying yourself, at a time like this? When will you get back?'

'I'm not sure. As soon as I can.'

'I should hope so.' Stooping beside the stained rug, she rolled it up and lifted it on to one hip with her strong arms.

'I'll clean this thing upstairs,' she said brusquely. 'Come to my sitting-room as soon as you get in tomorrow night.'

He promised to come. After all he was in her power. But he was more than ever determined to go to Charlotte Mitchell's house tomorrow evening. His way of escape, the only possible way open to him, lay through that house in Bruton Street and Miss Mitchell's money.

5

In New Bond Street next day Stephen talked to George Harris.

'I am supposed to be dining with you this evening, George,' he said.

Harris grinned. 'And who is the little lady?'

'That's my affair, I am afraid.'

'Quite so, old boy. But who is it that supposes you are dining with me? I ought to know, in case I ever have to lie on your behalf.'

'Kitty Daniels. You remember her at that place in Great Portland Street, I expect.'

'I do indeed. A charmer, if ever there was one.'

'By the way,' Stephen said, 'I want some information about travelling on the Continent.'

It was well known at the music shop that Harris had had several short continental holidays, and he was always pleased to talk about passports, language difficulties and French cooking.

'Take the little lady to Gay Paree,' he advised. 'No place like Gay Paree.'

Stephen smiled discreetly, got the information he needed and, on the whole, felt relieved. The enterprise that he had in mind was evidently less daunting than he had feared. It was Miss Fairford who had given him the idea. When she flung herself upon him in the music-room she had begged him to come abroad with her. It had been an awful moment. But the idea had stuck. He must get out of the country. Not alone, however, if he could help it. With good luck he would go as Charlotte Mitchell's husband.

If she refused, if she shrank back from the notion as a wild and imprudent step which she could not possibly contemplate, he would be obliged to go alone. But go somehow he must. Not for very much longer could he stay in the same country as that body in the cellar at Cassilis Street.

In the meanwhile Kitty must be kept in the dark, which was why he had had to prime George Harris about the alleged dinner. Kitty was not the easiest person to deceive, and she knew where to find Harris.

At Bruton Street that evening, Charlotte Mitchell had obviously gone to some pains to make herself look nice. He flattered her, delicately at first, then more boldly, laying it on thick.

Blushing and wriggling with pleasurable excitement in her spinsterish way, she said: 'Now you are being silly. Tell me what music you have brought this evening.'

He showed the music. 'This one is rather charming. One of H. W. Goodban's. *Moonlight on the Gondola*, it is called. I believe that it is supposed to catch the spirit of Venice perfectly.'

As he played it to Charlotte Mitchell, his mind gave him back with grim, inexorable fidelity the terrible scene that had followed the last time he had played the piece—Miss Fairford clawing at him, urging him to come abroad with her, anywhere he wished, at her expense.

When he had reached the last sentimental note, Charlotte Mitchell merely said: 'My parents took me abroad several times, but never to Venice.'

'You don't like the piece?'

'I like it pretty well. But I prefer *The Game of Love*, that you played the other night.'

There was a shy sort of invitation in her reply. Moving closer to her he took one of her hands in his, very tenderly, so as not to frighten her.

'Sitting here together,' he said, 'we might almost be husband and wife.'

'So we might,' she whispered.

'Would you like that, Charlotte?'

Looking down at her lap she said: 'Very much.'

It was over. The timid creature had been captured more easily than he could have believed. There had been no hesitations, no tears. She must have been more than ready for him to say the word. As he took her gently in his arms he murmured: 'Then I am the luckiest man in the world.'

The sense of a new freedom intoxicated him. Around him in the elegant music-room at Bruton Street were the signs of considerable wealth. And now it would be his.

All at once her face clouded. 'There are just one or two things that I hope you will agree to, Stephen.'

He waited, wondering what was coming, but prepared to agree to anything.

'I wish our marriage to be very quiet,' she went on. 'I shall say nothing to anyone. And I ask you to do the same. I want it to be our secret. You see, I dislike a fuss and I simply could not bear a fashionable wedding. It would kill me. I would rather not get married than have to endure all that—the people staring at me, and everything. Our marriage only concerns us, doesn't it? When it is over I shall write to my lawyer and tell him. Nothing else is really necessary . . . Another thing is that I don't wish to live in England. The climate doesn't suit me and I am never well here. I would much rather live on the Continent. When my parents used to take me abroad I didn't enjoy it because they never went to the sort of quiet, out-of-the-way spots that I like. Papa preferred gay, expensive resorts and the people whom one finds in such places.'

He made a show of resistance, though she could hardly have said anything that tallied with his own plans more completely.

'It would be splendid to be able to lead you down the aisle from the altar,' he mused. 'You would be wearing that bridal veil of your mother's, and I should be looking so proud and happy. But as you are so much against it——'

'It would make me miserable, Stephen, if not actually ill. Do you mind so dreadfully if we have a quiet, private wedding? It means so much to me.'

He reassured her. 'Whatever you like best will always be the thing that I like best.'

This little speech, which was the more effective for being sincere, seemed to convince her. She was all smiles again.

'And how about living abroad?' she said, as though, the chief obstacle overcome, she felt confident of getting her way on this point also.

'I have never been abroad. For me it would be a marvellous adventure.'

'You are sure that you won't mind leaving England?'

'Quite sure, dearest.'

She let him go at last, postponing the moment of parting again and again with small transparent excuses. As he went home he reflected that, barring accidents, he had secured his future magnificently. But it was just those accidents, of one sort or another, that he still had to fear. The prize was not yet won, and as long as he was in England, a false step could upset everything. Miss Fairford was lying in the floor-cloth in the recesses of the cellar. And Kitty was waiting for him in her room at Cassilis Street.

6

Kitty was not in the most amiable of moods.

'I'd practically given you up,' she grumbled. 'I must say it's a pretty fine thing, dining out in the West End when we've got all this on our hands. I was a goose to get mixed up in it. Still, it's done now and we've got to think of the next move.'

He accepted the reproof meekly. After the exciting evening in Bruton Street it was hateful to be plotting with a housemaid about the disposal of a corpse. But he couldn't afford to quarrel with Kitty.

'Has anything happened today?' he said, trying not to appear worried.

'Your father mentioned the old floor-cloth that we used last night. He was going to send a boy from the shop to take it away. I told him a junk man had called this morning and that I'd got rid of it that way. He seemed pleased. He would probably never have remembered to send the boy anyhow.'

Stephen braced himself to ask a vital question. 'Has anyone noticed yet that Miss Fairford is missing?'

'I wondered when you were going to ask me that.' She was still annoyed that he had absented himself that evening. 'Well, Nelly noticed, as you may suppose. But I shut her up pretty quick. Nobody else bothered . . . Now listen to me, Stephen. The story is that Miss Fairford left this morning in a cab at about eleven o'clock. Your father was out, of course. Your mother was out as well, doing some shopping. And your sister was at her school. Most of the lodgers were out too. In any case cabs often draw up here, as you know. One more or less makes no difference. I told Nelly that she wasn't to go to Miss Fairford's room this morning, as Miss Fairford didn't wish to be disturbed. About a quarter to eleven I sent Nelly out on an errand that would take her an hour or so. And in that time I got all Miss Fairford's things up to my room. I've got it all safe up here and I shall have to get rid of it by degrees. When your father came in I just told him that Miss Fairford had gone rather suddenly, leaving no forwarding address.'

'What did he say?'

'He said, "Good riddance," and asked if the rent was paid up to date. I said it was. He didn't even want to know why she had gone.'

Stephen moved closer to her, so that his knee touched hers. 'You are a marvel, Kitty.'

She melted. 'A good job you've got me to look after you.'

Somehow, after the nervous strain of the evening at Bruton Street, it was almost a relief to be with Kitty now. Their collaboration no longer seemed a hateful thing, as it had been when he first came in. He was as fond of her as ever. And she was without any doubt a feast for a man's sensual nature. Unfortunately he could not afford to give way to his sensual nature. He had his future to think of. And his future lay with Charlotte Mitchell.

For a while they did not talk. Then Kitty said: 'Well, now you know the story. If anyone asks you, you only know what I've told you. But I haven't been able to work out the most important thing yet. How are we going to get Miss Fairford away? I was puzzling over it when you came in.'

He was too tired to think. 'I don't know, Kitty. I've been worrying about it myself off and on all day.'

'We shall have to do something soon. She'll start to stink before long.'

The crudity made him flinch and Kitty's amused expression showed him that, after all, the gulf between them was still there.

'I'm sorry, Kitty,' he said. 'I must seem a useless creature. I'm afraid I don't shine in a situation of this kind.'

'You certainly don't. Anyhow, cheer up. We've done pretty well so far. I'll have to see what I can think of tomorrow.'

The next day Nelly went down with influenza.

'Caught it from one of her pals, I suppose,' Kitty complained. 'We shall all catch it now, mark my words. She goes into every room in the house for one thing or another. There's a lot of influenza about, I know, but we might have got off lightly if it hadn't been for her.'

After a few days the only person in the house who had caught the infection from Nelly was Kitty herself. She refused to go to bed or to have the doctor but she looked very sick, as she dragged herself doggedly round the house, attending to the things that could not be put off.

Stephen begged her to go to bed for a few days, but he might have saved his breath. She stuck to her post and gradually got over the worst of the bout. It left her weak, however.

'Kitty needs a holiday,' Mother remarked at supper one evening. 'She isn't herself at all.'

Stephen said nothing. Kitty wasn't likely to take a holiday as long as that roll of old floor-cloth was in the cellar.

Mother seemed quite concerned. 'I fancy that this influenza must have been coming on for some days before we knew about it,' she said. 'I remember that on the evening when we had been to the Sainsburys' and I saw Kitty in the music-room, she appeared to be very tired.'

To Stephen it was all like a bad dream. There was no enjoyment in life for him any longer, only a terrible anxiety, until the day when he would be across the Channel and travelling further and further away from the French coast.

About a fortnight after the disastrous evening in the music-room Mr and Mrs. Sainsbury came to return Mother and Dad's visit on that day. Stephen looked in to speak to the Sainsburys, whom he had known for most of his life. Old Sainsbury wasn't a bad sort. Better anyhow than his wife, who was apt to be a blight on any gathering at which she was present.

On this occasion she remarked: 'I suppose your drains are all right here?'

She was a pasty, dumpy woman, inclined to be dressy, though one felt that no amount of adornment could do much for her.

Her husband smiled indulgently. 'My better half is always fancying that she smells something disagreeable.'

'Well, Tom,' she protested. 'I do think that is quite uncalled-for. It was just that, as we were by the front door, I did smell something that made me wonder about the drains. It may have been something to do with the neighbours.'

She was invariably suspicious of neighbours. In her opinion, no neighbour was ever up to any good.

Dad said: 'Have you noticed anything, Edith?'

Mother hadn't, it appeared.

'So far as I know,' Dad observed, 'none of the lodgers has complained. But I will ask Kitty about that.'

Mrs. Sainsbury looked unconvinced. 'Well, its your house, not mine. But I did smell something as I came in.'

To Stephen, Mrs. Sainsbury's words were like a policeman's hand on his shoulder. Probably the smell wasn't very bad yet. But somebody had noticed it. Fortunately, all the time Miss Fairford had been in the cellar, the March days had been cold. The cellar, he remembered, had been icy on the night when he had been down there with Kitty.

The conversation moved round to the subject of a recent murder in a house not many streets away. A woman had been found stabbed and her husband had disappeared.

Tom Sainsbury said: 'If he has any sense he's skipped off abroad somewhere by now. Assuming that he did it, which I don't doubt.'

He spoke lightly, with a chuckle, as though the husband might conceivably be entitled to a certain sympathy.

Stephen, affecting a polite interest in a legal matter, said: 'What about extradition, Mr. Sainsbury? You would know all about that, as a lawyer.'

'Extradition isn't a matter I ever have to consider in the

office, my boy. There are certain extradition treaties, of course, as everyone knows. But after all, the man's got to be caught first, hasn't he? It isn't too difficult to lose yourself and your identity abroad, if you give your mind to it. And if you have a bit of money, that would make things even easier, I suppose.'

Afterwards Stephen regretted having raised the extradition question. It was just possible that it might be remembered against him later on. But the thing was done now. And old Sainsbury's remarks, for what they were worth, had on the whole been reassuring.

In those March days following Miss Fairford's death, Stephen led a double life. At Cassilis Street he behaved as though nothing had changed. In New Bond Street, to the surprise of his employers, he gave up his situation. After that he was mostly at Charlotte Mitchell's house in Bruton Street in the day-time.

Kitty was still suffering from the after-effects of the bout of influenza. Her light step was jaded and heavy, and she was irritable with him because he had done nothing about Miss Fairford.

'I just feel too tired to bother about corpses myself,' she said, 'so if anybody is going to get rid of the old dear, it'll have to be you, Stephen. And if you don't do something soon, we shall stand in the dock together before long and that'll be the end of us.'

He told her about Mrs. Sainsbury and the smell.

'She must have a good nose for a stink,' Kitty remarked. 'I haven't noticed anything myself. Though it's true I haven't been in the coal-cellar lately. And Nelly hasn't said anything. But the slut smells so strong herself sometimes that no other smell has a chance when she's about. All the same, the days are going on.'

Fantastic schemes occurred to him. He thought of disguising himself as a rag-and-bone man, hiring a horse and cart and, with Kitty's help, getting the body down to the river. Or he might manage with a hand-cart.

Kitty shook her head. 'You couldn't make yourself look like a rag-and-bone man. You'd be stopped by a policeman before you'd gone far.' She couldn't help laughing at the idea of her dapper Stephen pushing a hand-cart through London. 'I'd give something to see that, honest I would. Still, I shouldn't laugh. It's no laughing matter, God knows.'

In the end all he did was to go back to the cellars one night and pile a lot of the previous tenant's old rubbish on top of Miss Fairford. By that time he had given up hope of ever getting her out.

Meanwhile at Bruton Street events were moving towards a climax. Charlotte, he discovered, could be forceful and energetic enough when she had set her heart on something. There was, it seemed, more than a trace of her father and grandfather in her after all. Presumably she had never wanted something desperately before. Or, if she had, it had not been possible to achieve it in her parents' life-time.

But now, these frustrations swept away, she practically took command of the situation. Stephen was astonished to find that the ineffectual spinster had such a will of her own.

One day at Bruton Street she said: 'I don't like the name Berridge much, Stephen. And I'm not fond of Mitchell either. If I have to change my name on getting married, why shouldn't you?'

He was taken aback at first. It seemed such an extraordinary thing to do. Then, remembering Mr. Sainsbury's remarks about losing your identity in a foreign country, he said: 'As long as we are together, I don't mind what we are called.'

'That is so good of you, Stephen, so like you.'

'What name would you prefer?'

She had already thought of one. 'Bland,' she said. 'Mr. and Mrs. Stephen Bland. Don't you think that sounds nice? Bland was my grandmother's maiden name—my mother's mother. So it's a family name in a way.'

'How about the legal position?'

'Oh, legally we shall be Berridge. But to the world our name will be Bland. If we are going to start a new life together, a new name will be such a help, I feel. After a while I shall get my lawyer to do whatever seems necessary.'

Yes, she astonished him. Sometimes he wished that she had remained the spineless, insipid creature whose heart the young piano-tuner had captured. But he had to accept her as she was. He could not do without her now.

7

They were married so quietly that Charlotte was hardly nervous at all. Afterwards they went back to Bruton Street, and in the evening he turned up at Cassilis Street as though he had come home from work in the usual way.

That was a Tuesday. Early on the Friday morning they were to leave London.

It had to be a secret flitting. Stephen, even now, was to say nothing to anybody. Charlotte didn't actually insist on this. She merely asked him, pleading her shyness, if he would mind very much.

He was in an increasingly difficult position at Cassilis Street. If he left without saying anything, as Charlotte wished, there would be a hue and cry. Dad would go to the police, and if the police came to the house they might start rooting around in the cellars. On the other hand, if he told his parents the truth, Mother would certainly tell Kitty the news within the next hour. And Kitty would hardly take it lying down.

Eventually he hit upon a plan.

On the Wednesday he called at the shop to see Dad, who was in his counting-house. It was almost impossible to be sure of seeing Dad alone at home. But the counting-house at the shop was ideal for Stephen's purpose.

Dad was surprised. 'Hello, my boy, what are you doing here at this time of day?'

'I wanted to speak to you in confidence, Dad.'

Stephen noticed that his father looked away rather glumly. A request for a confidential chat sounded like trouble, and Dad disliked trouble.

'What is the matter, Stephen?' he asked, glancing at the clock as though he had not much time to spare.

'I shan't keep you long. The fact is that the firm want me to go to Paris. They have opened a branch there and as I am fairly young and unmarried they say that I should be a suitable man for the situation. Another man was to have gone but he backed out. His fiancée wouldn't hear of it apparently. I only learned about this definitely this morning, so I haven't mentioned it before. I do feel that it is an opportunity that I ought not to miss.'

Dad took a little while to consider this. 'I agree that you ought to go,' he said at length. 'It may lead to very material advancement. What about the language?'

'I am sure that I shall soon pick that up.'

'I expect you will. What I am not clear about is why you feel it necessary to come here and tell me this in confidence. Why not tell us all at home?'

Stephen began hesitantly, as though he were somewhat ashamed of what he had to say.

'I am afraid,' he said, 'that lately I have become too friendly with Kitty. These things start in a small way and by degrees they get out of hand. She wants me to marry her but I don't wish to go as far as that.'

Dad was looking embarrassed. 'I think you could do better than Kitty. An excellent woman in her way but hardly the wife for you. Marriage is a serious step.'

'That is how I feel, Dad. In the circumstances this offer by the firm has come as a positive godsend. But if Kitty knows about it before I go, she will want to come with me

Or she might try to stop my going. In any case there would be a terrible scene. I didn't know what to do. So I have come to you to find out whether you can help me.'

Dad was playing with a pen on his desk and frowning down at some papers. Finally with painful diffidence he said: 'Is Kitty in the family way?'

'Not as far as I am concerned. If she had been, I should have felt it my duty to marry her.'

'Certainly. But as the matter stands you are free to go as and when you please.' Dad seemed relieved. 'When do you go?'

'Tomorrow evening.'

'So soon? Well, the sooner the better, I suppose. Now let me see, how shall we manage this?' The pen went tap-tap on the desk. 'How about your travelling arrangements?'

'The firm will attend to all that. I have only to pack a valise and go.'

'If Kitty sees you leaving the house with a valise she may be suspicious.'

In the silence that followed their eyes met. They were no longer father and son now. They had become two males intent on hoodwinking a female.

'I think I have it,' Dad said. 'You had better leave at the usual time tomorrow morning. Say nothing to Mother or anybody. Call here on your way to New Bond Street. I will leave the house with the valise about ten minutes after you and take a cab to Tottenham Court Road as soon as I get round the corner. You will be waiting here at the shop and I shall hand over the valise to you. My leaving the house carrying a valise will not arouse any curiosity because, as you know, I often bring small bric-à-brac home from sales in a bag and take the stuff along to the shop later on . . . I assume that you will spend Thursday night in the train and on the boat.'

Stephen agreed that he would have to do this. 'I feel bad about leaving Mother without telling her,' he said.

'Oh, she will understand when I explain matters to her. Besides you aren't going for ever. We shall soon be seeing you again, I hope. And by that time Kitty may have found someone else. Or she may have left Cassilis Street.'

Dad seemed quite pleased, as though he was gratified that his son had had to come to him for help in this delicate and difficult matter.

'Now tell me about the position in Paris,' he added. 'It sounds interesting.'

'I know hardly anything about it myself as yet.'

'Well, you will be writing. We shall look forward to your letters. And I must say I think you were very wise to take the opportunity of disentangling yourself.'

They shook hands and Stephen said: 'Thanks for your help, Dad.'

'Very glad to have been of service, my boy.'

The plan succeeded. On the Thursday morning Stephen walked along to Tottenham Court Road from Cassilis Street and waited at the shop for Dad, who arrived within the next quarter of an hour with the valise. As Stephen left the shop and took a cab to Bruton Street, he felt like a fugitive from justice. Perhaps, he thought, that was exactly what he was. Even the valise was no more than dust in his parents' eyes, for at Bruton Street his new travelling clothes would be laid out for him. By this time tomorrow he would be on his way to the Continent. Mr. and Mrs. Stephen Bland would have started life together.

He no longer thought of his marriage merely as a gateway to the affluent, gentlemanly life. It was primarily as a way of escape that it was valuable to him now. Escape from prison, possibly from the gallows.

Dad and Ruth meant little to him, but leaving Mother was painful. Leaving Kitty was more painful still, because he was leaving her in the lurch. She was the only person, other than himself, who knew about Miss Fairford. Whatever happened now, she would bear the brunt of it. He couldn't forgive himself and he didn't try.

At Bruton Street all the arrangements were made. Very early next morning they were to leave the house and catch the 7.15 at Victoria, travelling to Dover on the London, Chatham and Dover line. The sea passage would take about an hour and a half. Charlotte was excited but inclined to be fearful. It was a journey into the unknown and, now that she had come to the brink, she needed comfort and reassurance.

He gave her both. She was, after all, giving him so much.

They were in good time for the train that Friday morning. Later in the day Stephen, wearing a new travelling cap pulled down over his ears, and a heavy overcoat with a cape and a high collar, stood for a while on deck and watched the coast of England recede into the mist.

By six o'clock, according to the time-table, they would be in Paris.

4

I

EDITH BERRIDGE had been the only child of an unsuccessful grocer. Both her parents were recently dead when she met John Berridge, and Aunt Sophy at Windsor was now almost her only living relative. She had sometimes thought that it was partly this general absence of relatives that had commended her to him, at the time when he was contemplating a second marriage, for he was not a sociable man. At the chapel he was considered to be aloof and severe in manner, but it was generally agreed that his style was dignified.

She doubted whether he had ever been in love with her. As for her own feelings, all she could be sure of was that she had never been sorry that she had married him. He was considerate and, as far as his business allowed, regular in his habits. He did not get drunk.

He was, of course, inclined to be susceptible to the charms of other women. She found that out a year or two after their marriage. But by that time she had grown to be fond of him and used to him. She knew him well enough by then to feel reasonably certain that he wasn't the sort of man who would leave his wife and his home, however infatuated he might be. Events proved her right. In the end he always got tired of his new love. While he was in the toils she looked the other way. She was jealous, as any woman would be. But she was sensible too and did not make a fuss that would only have fanned the flame.

Probably he supposed that she was never aware of these escapades of his. The air of simplicity with which she faced the world deceived him, as it deceived most people. She had never tried to deceive anybody, in point of fact. It was just that nature had given her the sort of appearance that goes with innocence. But she had had to hold her own in life, and she hadn't been able to do that without losing much of whatever simplicity she had started out with.

Seeing her husband about to leave the house that Thursday morning with a valise which she recognised as Stephen's, she was on the point of asking where he was going with it, but stopped herself in time. John did not like questions of that sort. Taking no notice of the valise she said: 'Home for dinner at the usual time, dear?'

'About as usual, I expect,' he replied as he went out.

She felt sad, without really knowing why. Perhaps it was because there had been something ever so slightly guilty in his manner, something that their years together had taught her to recognise. Wondering what it was that he was keeping from her, she sat down and took up some needlework. She did a good deal of needlework, mainly for the chapel, where there was always a demand for it at the periodical Sales of Work.

There was a ring at the tradesmen's bell down in the area. Looking out, she saw that it was the greengrocer. Very often he sent his boy, but today he had come himself. Presently she could hear Kitty's voice, and the expression on the greengrocer's face became lively and amorous. Kitty had that effect on men.

Edith had started by liking Kitty. Now she merely depended on her, while still maintaining a vigorous pretence of liking. There was, Edith regretfully acknowledged to herself, a weak side to her own nature. She knew that she ought not to depend on Kitty Daniels as she did. It gave the woman more power than was proper. But if Kitty were to leave, the consequences would be most disagreeable. To begin with,

John, who was very much in Kitty's pocket, would be upset. Then perhaps there would be trouble with Stephen, whose fondness for Kitty was all too obvious. And finally she herself would probably have to run the lodging-house, and she was afraid that she would do it badly.

So the months had gone by and she had turned a blind eye to things, taking herself off periodically to Aunt Sophy's house at Windsor when she felt that she needed the refreshment of a change.

When John came in for dinner at one o'clock on that unhappy Thursday, he said: 'Stephen won't be in for supper this evening.'

'He didn't mention it,' she pointed out gently.

'He didn't know when he left this morning. The firm asked him to go out somewhere today. A special job in the country, I understood. Stephen won't be able to get back in time for supper. He sent a message to me by a man who had to come up Tottenham Court Road and would be passing the shop.'

Ruth, who was listening, said: 'Stephen has been out somewhere or other in the evening a great deal lately, it seems to me.'

John ignored this remark, and Edith merely smiled absent-mindedly, wondering about Stephen's valise.

After dinner, when Ruth had gone back to Miss Picknett's, John said: 'I am sorry, Edith. That wasn't true about Stephen.'

Her heart seemed to miss a beat, as though her palpitations were coming on.

'What is wrong, John?' she managed to say.

'Nothing is wrong. But I didn't want to talk in front of Ruth. The fact is that Stephen, quite unexpectedly, has had the chance to go to Paris for the firm. It may be a big thing for him.'

'How long will he be away?'

'He wasn't sure. But it wasn't just a flying visit.'

She was nearly in tears. 'I don't understand. Why didn't he tell us? What does all this mean?'

Her husband glanced over his shoulder as if to make certain that the door was shut. Then, in a low voice, he said: 'It is because of Kitty. As you know, they have been getting much too intimate. Now she is on at him to marry her and he doesn't want to. I don't blame him either. He can do a lot better than Kitty Daniels. Well, yesterday he came to see me privately at the shop.' He went on to relate the details of the plot for getting Stephen out of the house without Kitty knowing. 'So that's that, my dear,' he concluded. 'I wasn't sure whether I should have a chance of seeing you alone this dinner-time, so I thought I had better invent that story about the job in the country for the time being.'

She was hurt and bewildered. That Stephen should have gone off in this way, slinking out, taking his father into his confidence and keeping her out of it—it was dreadful. She couldn't believe it. There must be something else behind it, she felt.

'I suppose Stephen will be writing?' she ventured.

'Of course. As soon as he is settled.'

'And what are we to tell Kitty? We shall have to tell her something. From what you say, he isn't likely to write to her himself.'

He hesitated. 'You had better tell her that Stephen had to go at a moment's notice. After all it is practically true, isn't it?'

'I am not very good at not telling the truth, John . . . You did say that I was to tell Kitty, did you?'

'It would come better from you, I think.' He looked at his watch. 'I must be getting back.'

When she was alone she went upstairs and cried for a while. Really men did put a terrible strain on the affections of women. John had gone sneaking off like a coward, leaving her to face Kitty. As for Stephen, she could still not believe that he could have left without kissing her good-bye. And not only that. He and John had deliberately deceived her, concocting a scheme together to pull the wool over her eyes.

In her grief and anger she felt sorry for Kitty. The woman was not to be trusted with men, but one had to remember that females in her position had many temptations. Whatever her faults she was fond of Stephen—in love with him, one might even say—and it was very wrong of the boy to run away as he had done, just because he thought Kitty wasn't good enough for him.

It was a sorry tale, all of it. And it wasn't finished yet. She had to tell Kitty the truth. No, not the truth. That in a way would have been easier. But John would be very annoyed if she told Kitty the truth. Besides, how could one be quite sure that John's story was indeed the whole truth of the matter?

It was best, it seemed, to say what would spare Kitty's feelings for the time, leaving her to find out the truth, whatever it was, by degrees.

Edith wiped her eyes, washed her face and sat back quietly in her chair for ten minutes to compose herself for the coming encounter. She had the advantage that Kitty, like most people, probably thought her a simpleton. It would never occur to Kitty that kind Mrs. Berridge might be trying to deceive her.

When she felt sufficiently calm, she went up to Kitty's sitting-room. It was rarely that she ascended to the attic floor, because of her heart.

Kitty was in her armchair, apparently examining a lace collar closely, as if to make sure that it had no flaws. She looked up with a startled face.

'Why, Kitty, what a pretty collar!' Edith was in no hurry to get on to the topic that had brought her to Kitty's room. 'It is rather like the collars that that queer Miss Fairford used to wear sometimes.'

'As a matter of fact Miss Fairford gave me this as a sort of parting present, ma'am. She had some nice clothes, I will say that.'

'Relics of better days, I suppose.'

'I suppose so . . . You gave me quite a start, coming in like that, ma'am. It isn't often I see you up here. I wondered what could have happened.'

'Nothing has happened. At least, nothing very dreadful.' Edith seated herself with deliberation. 'I don't really know why I came up to tell you, except that, as you say, I so rarely do come up here to see you. Anyhow, I thought I would do so this afternoon . . . Well now, it is just this. Mr. Berridge told me at dinner-time that Mr. Stephen has been sent away on business by his firm at a moment's notice. Mr. Stephen was able to get a message to his father. But that was all he was able to do. However, he will no doubt be writing soon, and then we shall know more about it. I thought I would tell you now, because of Stephen's supper this evening. And of course it did occur to me that you and Stephen might have had an arrangement to go out somewhere together in the near future. It is all most inconvenient, and I really do not understand why the firm could not have given him proper notice. However, Mr. Berridge says that it may be very good for Mr. Stephen's prospects, so I suppose we must look at it in that way.'

It was unnaturally quiet in Kitty's room, like a room in a street where straw has been put down because of somebody who is ill. Kitty herself looked suddenly white and drawn. She was crumpling the pretty collar in her hands.

'Where has Mr. Stephen gone, ma'am?' she said at last.

'To Paris, Mr. Berridge said.'

'Paris! But what would he be doing in Paris?'

'Mr. Berridge wasn't certain, but it seems that it was in connection with a branch that is being opened by the firm there.'

Kitty's eyes were dark with suspicion. 'Why didn't he send a message here, instead of to Mr. Berridge?'

'I don't know, Kitty. Perhaps he hadn't time.'

'Do you mean that Mr. Stephen is already on his way?'

'I was told that he had to go at a moment's notice.'

'Surely he must have had some idea before. Why didn't he say nothing? But perhaps he did say something to you, ma'am——'

'He did not, Kitty. It was as big a shock to me as it is to you. Frankly I don't understand it.' Then, feeling that she had done enough for John she added: 'If you want to know any more, I am afraid that you will have to ask Mr. Berridge this evening.'

'Very well, ma'am. I will do that. You don't know how long Mr. Stephen will be away, do you?'

'I have no notion at all. Still, Mr. Berridge says that Mr. Stephen will be writing. Perhaps there will be a letter for you in a few days.'

Kitty nodded dully. 'Thank you for telling me, ma'am.'

Edith closed the door quietly behind her, glad that the conversation was over. It had not been so very dreadful, though Kitty was obviously shaken.

Going downstairs she thought in a random way about that pretty collar. A strange present for Miss Fairford to have given Kitty. But she had been a strange person. One had felt sorry for the old lady, but also rather relieved when she took herself off.

2

As soon as John came in that evening, he said: 'Well, did you tell Kitty?'

Edith was hanging up his overcoat for him. 'I told her this afternoon.'

'How did she take it?'

'It was a shock.'

'She'll get over it. I suppose she wanted chapter and verse for everything.'

'She certainly did want to know more than I could tell

her. She is going to ask you for more details tonight. Have you heard anything further?'

'No, I didn't expect to yet.'

'We must tell Ruth,' said Edith.

'I hardly think that Ruth will bother herself much about it.'

At supper Ruth said: 'Is Stephen going to be out very late tonight?'

John affected a casual, matter-of-fact tone. 'We find now that Stephen will be away for a little time. He has been sent to the firm's branch in Paris.'

'Paris! How lovely!'

'He had to step into another man's shoes at a moment's notice. We know very little about it now, but his letters will no doubt tell us everything in due course.'

The casual tone had become firm and final. He wanted no more questions and Ruth understood this.

'How did school go today, dear?' Edith asked her.

'About as usual, Mother. I tried to get the three dunces to spell some extremely simple words again, but it was no good.'

'It will come all at once, I expect.'

'I don't know. Perhaps I am just a bad teacher. I shall have to give it up and get married, like other girls.'

'I hope,' Edith said, 'that you will indeed get married, Ruth, when the right man comes along.'

When supper was over and Ruth had gone upstairs, they talked about Stephen again.

'He could be as close as wax when he liked,' John said.

'But, John, you don't think that he is concealing something, do you?'

'I have no particular reason to think that. I merely said that on occasion he could be as close as wax.'

It was evident that John, whatever he might say to the contrary, was himself beginning to wonder whether there might not be more in this Paris journey than met the eye.

Presently he went upstairs to see Kitty. When he returned, he said: 'That woman missed her vocation. She ought to have been a barrister.'

'My dear, how could Kitty ever have become a barrister?'

'She couldn't, of course. I know that. But she behaved like a Q.C. this evening, I can tell you. Talk about searching questions—I hope I never have to submit to anything like it in the witness box.'

'Now, John, why should you ever have to go into a witness box?'

'One never knows. The witness box isn't like the dock. Well, as I say, Kitty questioned me like one of the clever lawyers that you read about in the reports of criminal cases in the papers. You know, trying to make me contradict myself, and so on. By the time I left her I felt like a criminal myself. She's got a good brain, that woman. If she had been a man, there's no telling what she might have done.'

From the street there came an inarticulate clamour, the sound of hurrying footsteps and men's voices shouting: 'Stepney murder! Latest! Stepney murder!'

John listened. 'Running patterers,' he said at length. 'Selling their broadsheets, poor devils, or trying to. They have to be in advance of the papers if they can. They earn as much as a pound a week sometimes, I've been told, but more often it's nearer five shillings. Anyhow it provides them with a bed for the night.'

'Always a murder somewhere in London,' Edith sighed.

It was by no means the first time that running patterers had come up Cassilis Street in the evening. There were generally two, three or four men, and they divided up—two on each pavement if there were four of them. Some of the lodgers, hearing the patterers in the street, occasionally came down to the front door and bought a broadsheet for a penny or a halfpenny, but Edith had never done so. She was sorry for the poor fellows. But they really ought to make an effort to get regular employment and not live on the streets.

'I suppose,' she said, 'if we don't hear from Stephen we could call at the shop in New Bond Street and find out the address in Paris.'

'We shall hear from Stephen all right,' he assured her confidently, 'You must give him a few days.'

3

They gave Stephen a few days. They gave him, in the end, ten wretched days of listening for the postman's knock.

Edith tried to behave as though she had nothing disagreeable on her mind, and John seemed to be doing the same, but they were both uneasy, and occasionally snapped at each other and at Ruth. Kitty went about looking as if she had not slept properly the night before.

At last Edith had had enough of it. 'We really must go to New Bond Street, John, and get that address.'

'Very well, my dear. But there is no need for you to go. I am quite ready to go by myself.'

'No, John. I should like to be there too.'

'As you please. What about tomorrow morning?'

'Yes, if there is no letter by the first post.'

There was no letter and they set out together. 'I shall have a bone to pick with Master Stephen when I see him again,' John said.

'Oh, never mind that, dear. I only pray that he is safe and well.'

At the music establishment in New Bond Street, John explained their business to the polite young shopman who came forward.

The young man seemed puzzled, but all he said was: 'If you will kindly be seated, I will enquire of Mr. Gerrard.'

When he came back, he said: 'Will you step this way please.'

They followed him through the shop and up a staircase to a room on the first floor, where an affable, rather florid man advanced towards them with outstretched hand.

'I understand,' he began, 'that you are Mr. Stephen Berridge's parents. Am I correct?'

'Perfectly correct,' John told him.

'And I am further informed by my assistant that you wish to know the address of our firm's branch in Paris. Is that so?'

'That is so. My son was transferred to the Paris branch ten days ago, and so far we have not heard from him.'

Mr. Gerrard screwed up his eyes. 'He told you that, did he?'

'He did.'

'Did you not ask him for the address before he left? Surely he would have known it?'

John was visibly taken aback. 'I suppose he would. But he said that he had been transferred at a moment's notice, in place of a man who had backed out. He told me that he would be writing in a day or two.'

'You didn't go to the railway station with him?'

'No. It all happened in such a hurry.' John's tone was impatient now. 'May I ask the object of these questions, sir?'

'Certainly you may, Mr. Berridge . . . The fact is that your son was not transferred to Paris. Indeed, we have no shop in Paris.'

Edith's heart was pounding. 'Then where is he?' she burst out. 'What has happened to him?'

'I do not know where he is, madam, or what has happened to him. All I can tell you is that he left our service about three weeks ago. We were very sorry, because he was a most valued employee.'

The man's smooth manner faintly irritated her. 'Didn't he tell you where he was going to?'

'No. We naturally questioned him on the point, as we

should have liked him to stay, but he would tell us nothing.'

She looked across at John, but John was staring at the floor in a baffled sort of way.

'I assume,' said Mr. Gerrard, 'that you will report the matter to the police?'

'I haven't thought about that yet,' John said.

'Well, sir, we have your son's last address. In Cassilis Street I seem to remember. Is that also your own address?'

'Yes. The same address.'

'If we hear anything, we will notify you at once. The whole business is most disturbing, for us as well as for you.'

For the time being, there seemed to be nothing more to say.

Mr. Gerrard rang a bell and they were ushered out.

On the way back they hardly spoke. Edith's heart was still behaving as it often did after any exertion. There had been no physical exertion today but the emotional strain had been considerable.

Home at last, John flung himself into a chair and said: 'The young devil!'

'Now, John dear——'

'He made a fool of me.'

'There must be some misunderstanding. It isn't like Stephen at all.'

'Isn't it? I am beginning to think that I didn't know him very well. I always thought he was close, but I could never have believed that he would play his own father a trick like that.'

Edith was suffering miserably. A whole world seemed to have ended for her. All their years together, there had never been a cross word between Stephen and herself. Or hardly ever. She had brought him up as tenderly as if he had been her own son.

'There must be a mistake,' she mourned, beginning to cry. 'Some dreadful mistake——'

The stern lines on John's face softened. 'Don't upset yourself, Edie.' He came over to where she sat and put an arm round her shoulders. 'I suppose the truth is that he got into some sort of trouble and he was afraid to tell us about it.'

She leaned against him for comfort. 'The man said that he left three weeks ago. That means that for the first ten days, when we thought that he was going to the shop as usual, he was really going somewhere else . . . Where do you suppose he was, John?'

'I haven't a notion. I am simply out of my depth in all this. All I know for certain is that he lied himself black in the face. And even got me to help him. He was afraid of something. That is why I think that he was in some trouble or other.'

'Are you going to the police, as the man suggested?'

'No. Not yet, at any rate.'

'Aren't you supposed to report it when somebody disappears?'

'I'm not sure. In any case, I'm not going to report it yet. After all, Stephen might still turn up. It's only ten days. Or we might get a letter. The chances are that he is still in England somewhere. Of course, if he did get himself into a scrape, dangerous enough to make him run for it, the police may come here before we go to them.'

She fumbled for her handkerchief. 'What a dreadful affair it all is!'

'Shall we tell Kitty now? Or wait?'

'Do we need to tell her at all, John?'

'She might be able to help.'

They decided to tell her that evening, if no letter or message had come from Stephen during the day.

4

Nothing did come that day. After supper, when Ruth was out of the way, Edith said: 'I expect Kitty is in the kitchen now, John.'

John got up and went out, but was soon back again. 'Kitty will be here in a few minutes,' he said. Then, as though it was a relief to talk about something other than Stephen's disappearance, he added: 'I noticed that smell in the area as I came in this evening. The one that Mrs. Sainsbury mentioned. It seemed to come from the direction of the cellars. The drains run underneath, so no doubt that is the trouble. If it is I shall have to get in touch with the landlord.'

She doubted whether John would in fact approach the landlord. He was much more likely to do nothing and hope that the smell would pass off.

'Kitty hasn't said anything about it to me, John.'

'It isn't very bad, but if it gets worse we shall be obliged to find out what's wrong.'

She agreed perfunctorily. The drains were such a small matter by comparison with the mystery of Stephen's conduct.

When Kitty came in, John asked her to sit down and said: 'We think that you may be able to help us, Kitty.'

He proceeded to tell her about the interview with the man at the music shop that morning. Edith admired the way he did it, so lucidly, using all the right words. She herself would not have done it half as well.

Kitty listened. She was subdued this evening. You might almost have taken her manner for indifference.

'So he never went to Paris?' she said.

'No. At least, he didn't go as an employee of the firm.'

'It was all a pack of lies?'

'I am afraid so.'

She turned to Edith. 'Why should he have told a pack of lies, ma'am?'

'That's what we don't know, Kitty. We wondered whether you might be able to throw any light on it. Did he talk to you about any friends who might perhaps know more than we do?'

'No, ma'am. He never talked to me about his friends. Mr. Stephen wasn't the sort of young man who went about much with other young men, I should say.'

'Nobody at the shop?'

'Not that I can think of. He wasn't much of a talker, except about music. And what he was going to do if he was ever rich. That sort of talk, if you know what I mean.'

John leaned forward as though something had interested him. 'And what was he going to do if he became rich?'

'Well, you know, Mr. Berridge . . . Have a house in the country and servants and horses et cetera. And a big music-room where he could play and entertain his guests.'

'And where were these riches coming from?'

'I could never make that out. But anyhow I never took it seriously, and I don't reckon he ever meant it seriously either. Still, Mr. Stephen was ambitious, you can't deny that. I suppose the big talk about being rich was part of it.'

John sat back. 'I expect you are right. By the way, wasn't there a fellow called George Harris at the shop, that Stephen was friendly with?'

'Yes. There was a fellow called Harris. But I shouldn't think Mr. Stephen would have told him anything.'

'Is he still at the shop, do you know?'

'Couldn't say, Mr. Berridge. Only set eyes on him once in my life.'

John got up from his chair. 'Well, thank you, Kitty. It appears that you know no more than we do about this unhappy affair.'

'Afraid not. Unhappy it is, as you say. Him telling you

all those lies . . . Will there be anything else?'

Edith said that there would be nothing more that evening. 'And try to get a good night's sleep tonight, Kitty. You don't look yourself at all.'

Kitty went off with a shadowy smile and an apathetic good-night.

'Do you think she knows more than she is letting on?' John said, when Kitty had gone.

'She may, dear. But I feel sure that she doesn't know where Stephen is. It was so obviously a surprise to her when I told her that he had gone to Paris, that day when you asked me to break the news to her. She was shocked. And she hasn't been right since.'

John fiddled with his watch-chain. 'I must go to New Bond Street and see that fellow Harris,' he said at length. 'I'll go tomorrow.'

After breakfast next day he asked Edith whether she wished to come to New Bond Street with him.

'Not this time, John.' She felt that she couldn't face another ordeal so soon. 'You must tell me what happens when you come back.'

'Very good.' He paused at the door. 'I have been thinking about what Kitty said last night—about Stephen becoming rich and what he was going to do if he ever had plenty of money. Is it possible, my dear, that he can have been involved in a robbery or a swindle of some kind?'

She winced. 'Surely not.'

'There was something that sent him off in a great hurry. And his talents weren't of the sort that make a lot of money for a man.'

When John had gone, she picked up some needlework and drifted gently into a day-dream in which she was back in the small house off Gray's Inn Road, and Stephen, about ten years old, was coming in from school, and she could hear his voice calling her . . . *Ma! I say, Ma!* . . . She could hear him as plainly as if he had been in the room with her now. A nice boy he had been at that age. A pity that boys grew into men and, sometimes, became almost strangers.

The worst thing that Stephen could have been doing, she was sure, was gambling. She did not approve of gambling but it was at least better than robbing or swindling. And young men did quite often incur gambling debts.

In her own mind she decided that she had hit on the truth. Gambling had been the trouble. Stephen had been foolish, but not worse than foolish. There had been, one supposed, what men idiotically called a debt of honour. He had been unable to pay up, had taken fright, and was probably somewhere abroad by now.

These reflections consoled her. It was naughty of him to have told so many lies. But in her heart he was still a boy, and boys did tell lies, and one forgave them.

The second post brought a letter from Aunt Sophy at Windsor. Aunt Sophy had had one of her attacks of loneliness. She wanted Edith to go and stay with her for a few days. It wasn't long since the last visit to Windsor and Edith was wondering whether John would object to her going again so soon, when she heard John's footsteps in the hall.

'Well?' she said, as he came in.

'I saw this young Harris.' John lowered himself into his armchair. 'He was unwilling to talk at first. Then after a while he did say that one day last month Stephen had mentioned that they were supposed to be dining together that evening. Harris was to tell Kitty Daniels this if she ever asked questions. Harris knew Kitty slightly, you see, through Stephen. It was pretty obvious, Harris said, that Stephen was meeting another lady and didn't want Kitty to know. Nothing very unusual in that, of course. But it appears that Stephen went on to ask Harris about going to the Continent. Harris has been abroad several times on holiday and knows the ropes. He said that he told Stephen what he knew and thought no more about it at the time.'

'Did this Mr. Harris know why Stephen wanted the information?'

'Not exactly. Stephen gave him the impression that he was considering a holiday on the Continent himself. Putting two and two together, my dear, it certainly looks as if Stephen may have gone abroad with a woman.'

'But what woman could it possibly have been?'

'A woman that Kitty knew nothing about. A woman that we knew nothing about either. I doubt whether young Harris had any idea who it was.'

John did not go to business that day until after dinner. When he had gone, Edith went to look for Kitty and told her the result of John's interview with Harris, omitting the part relating to the lie that Stephen must have told Kitty about dining with Harris, when he had evidently been spending the evening in some other way. Kitty must find that out for herself, if she ever did find out.

'Mr. Berridge came to the conclusion,' Edith said, 'that Stephen has gone abroad, though we can't think why. The whole matter is a complete mystery.'

'I reckon Mr. Berridge is about right,' said Kitty, in a flat sort of voice.

'My idea is that Stephen has been gambling and has found himself unable to pay a debt of honour, as I think it would be called.'

'You may be right, ma'am.'

'Did he ever talk to you about gambling?'

'Not that I recollect. He never seemed that kind of man. But he wouldn't be likely to tell me everything, would he? Men get up to all manner of nonsense and say nothing about it. Till they're found out.'

Kitty sounded as if she had made up her mind about Stephen and had accepted the fact that she had lost him.

'Whatever the reason was,' Edith said severely, 'he had no right to go off like that.'

'No more he hadn't, ma'am . . . If you'll excuse me now I must run down to the kitchen.'

That night in the privacy of their bedroom Edith said: 'What are we going to tell people, John?'

'What people do you mean?'

'The people at the chapel. And the lodgers here—some of them are bound to ask where Stephen is. I think we had better tell them all that he had an opportunity of bettering himself. It meant going abroad and we don't expect to see him again for a long time. He took a situation as a traveller—that will be best. Not the ordinary sort of traveller, but one who has to travel in foreign parts.'

He nodded approvingly. 'But what about Kitty? She knows that we haven't a notion where he is.'

'Kitty is the only one who knows that. And I feel sure that she will keep her mouth shut. I may be wrong, but that is how I feel about her. She won't do anything to make things difficult for us.'

'I hope you're right.' His tone was resigned rather than hopeful. 'The men at the shop in New Bond Street all know that there is something wrong, of course. It isn't likely that Mr. Gerrard would have said anything, but the shopman we saw first yesterday would have discussed it with the others, including Harris. Still, these things blow over. We had better stick to your story about Stephen being a traveller abroad.'

She shrank from the prospect of deceit that seemed to stretch endlessly before her, even though she had suggested the lie herself.

At the end of another week there was no letter and she decided that she ought to go to Windsor to relieve Aunt Sophy's loneliness. In fact she wanted to go. Her mind was preying on itself in Cassilis Street.

'Kitty will look after you,' she told John. She added, as she generally did: 'Would you like to come with me this time? Aunt Sophy would be most pleased to see you.'

He declined. 'I'll stay and take care of Ruth,' he said gloomily. 'Before we know where we are she'll be skipping off like her brother.'

'Really, John, what a thing to say!'

'Well, after all, my dear, a few weeks ago Stephen seemed as steady and settled as Ruth. And see what happened!'

Edith enjoyed the few days at Windsor. Aunt Sophy was getting old but still liked toddling round the town, especially when she had somebody to go with. And at Windsor there were always delicious tit-bits of news about royalty, that did not get into general circulation. The atmosphere of tea and macaroons and talk in Aunt Sophy's parlour exactly suited Edith. It was a haven in which she would willingly have anchored, if duty had not called her elsewhere.

Duty, when she got back to Cassilis Street, met her with a slap in the face.

'I've got some bad news,' John said.

Her heart fluttered. 'Stephen?'

'No. Nothing about Stephen at all. Except indirectly, I suppose. Kitty gave me a week's notice last night.' He stared moodily at the mantelpiece. 'She wouldn't say why, except that she wanted a change. But of course it's plain enough that this business about Stephen has upset her. What we are going to do now I simply can't imagine.'

Edith thought wistfully of the peace of Windsor, Aunt Sophy's pleasant parlour. For a moment everything seemed as bad as it could be. Then she rallied.

'I'll speak to Kitty,' she said.

'It won't do any good, my dear. Kitty's mind is made up, unless I am very much mistaken.'

'One can but try.'

She tried next morning. 'Whatever is this I hear, Kitty?' she began.

Kitty understood. 'I'm sorry, ma'am.'

'There is nothing wrong here, is there? If it is a question of your wages——'

'The wages are quite all right, ma'am. As I told Mr. Berridge, I feel that I should like a change.'

'And what are we going to do without you?'

'I expect you'll find someone else pretty soon.'

'No one anything like as good as you, Kitty.'

'It's nice of you to say so, Mrs. Berridge, and I'm sure I'm glad to have given satisfaction. But I think I've been here long enough.'

Edith felt desperate.

'As a favour to me, Kitty,' she pleaded, 'will you stay on for a few weeks? Or perhaps until we have found somebody to take your place. Nobody could ever really take your place, I know that. But we may be able to get someone to do a part of the work that you have done. And perhaps I myself shall have to learn to take charge of the lodgers. I ought to have done it from the first, I suppose. But you did it so much better than I could possibly have done, that I left it to you. You have always been so obliging, Kitty. Would you please oblige me this last time? I should be very grateful if you would.'

Kitty hesitated. Her eyes were full of trouble, but there were no tears in them.

At last Edith said: 'Don't make your mind up at once. Take a little while to think it over.'

'I don't properly know what to say, ma'am. You see, my mind is made up as it is. I don't need time to make it up. But I tell you what. I will stay for a month. That'll give you a chance.'

Edith grasped the month with eager hands. It was better than the original week. Also, if Kitty stayed for a month, she might well stay longer.

'Thank you very much, Kitty,' she said humbly. 'Somehow I felt that you would not be hard on me. We have always got on so well together, haven't we?'

'Yes, ma'am, we have that.'

'Never a cross word.'

'That's right, ma'am.'

When Kitty had gone Edith drifted over to the window and gazed absent-mindedly at the traffic: the old doctor in Regent Square being driven to his patients in a brougham; a young doctor from Judd Street driving himself round in a gig; a carriage and pair; tradesmen's vehicles of all sorts.

She felt pleased with herself. She had succeeded where John had not even tried. Kitty would be staying for another month. It seemed, at that moment, as good as a year.

5

I

Kitty stayed on for three months, until mid-July. John Berridge had little to do with her during that time and never once went up to her room. Edith, on the other hand, was taking a much greater interest in the running of the house, against the day when Kitty would go.

'I don't think she will go at all now,' he told Edith one evening. 'She has got over the restless fit.'

'Oh yes, she will go, John. She has made up her mind to it. She is only staying for a while to oblige us.'

'I don't see why she has to leave. She has got a place here worth a good deal more to her than anything else that she is likely to get.'

'She has never been the same since Stephen went. She wants to go somewhere fresh, and if she was so attached to him, I can't say that I blame her.'

They still had no idea where Stephen was. No letter came, no message, nothing whatever. Not even the police came, so that at least it seemed that he had not got into serious trouble. Or if he had, the police did not know about it.

John Berridge began to give up thinking much about his son. In a way life was easier without him in the house. Stephen had been a perpetual reminder of Margaret, the first Mrs. Berridge, not only in his features and his stocky figure but in his disposition. That young Berridge couple years ago had been a quarrelsome pair. All the same he had loved

Margaret very dearly, and life lost much of its savour after her death.

Edith tried without success to find a housekeeper who would, to some extent, take Kitty's place when she left.

Eventually it was Kitty herself who solved the problem.

Early in July she informed Edith that, the previous evening, she had met a certain Lizzie Siddle in Great Ormond Street.

'Apparently,' Edith told John afterwards, 'this Lizzie Siddle had been a housemaid at Mrs. Thomson's house in Brunswick Square, the place where you first met Kitty. Lizzie Siddle and Kitty were there together for a time, so Kitty knows something about her. Lizzie is in service in Great Ormond Street at present but she isn't happy there and is looking round for something else. Kitty thought Lizzie would be the sort that we need here, so she spoke to Lizzie about it. Lizzie liked the idea but didn't wish to do the work in connection with the lodgers that Kitty has been doing, interviewing them when they come to the door, collecting the rents and so forth. I should do all that myself.'

'We shall have to see Lizzie Siddle first,' he said. He did not really want to lose Kitty, even though he no longer desired to go up to her room. 'I can't understand,' he grumbled, 'why Kitty has to put us to all this trouble. It's a lot of silly nonsense, her wanting to go.'

Edith was mild and sensible. 'Well, that is Kitty's business, dear. We can't keep her against her will.'

'You had better get the woman to call here.'

'I'll ask Kitty to arrange it. I expect Lizzie will be free on Sunday evening . . . I can't help thinking, John, that if Kitty is recommending Lizzie, we shall get on pretty well.'

Berridge secretly hoped that Edith would take a dislike to Lizzie Siddle, but his hopes were dashed when Lizzie called on the Sunday evening.

Edith talked to the woman for half an hour, then reported to her husband.

'I think she will do, John,' she said. 'Would you like to see her?'

'I suppose I had better.'

Lizzie Siddle proved to be a rather plain woman in the thirties with mousy hair screwed up carelessly under her chip bonnet. She had a dry, matter-of-fact way and a habit of sniffing. She was not talkative.

He asked her whether she had had a similar situation before.

'No, sir.'

'Kitty told you what was required, did she?'

'Yes, sir. And Mrs. Berridge did.'

'And you think that you can do all the work?'

'Oh, yes, sir. With the same help that Kitty has had, of course. But I understand that I shan't have anything to do with letting the rooms or collecting the rents.'

'Well, we will give it a trial, Lizzie. We shall need a character, of course.'

'Yes, sir. Thank you, sir.'

She smiled briefly and went out with Edith. Presently Edith was back.

'I am sure that we have an excellent woman there,' she said.

'I hope you are right.' He was not deeply interested.

It was arranged that Lizzie should come for a few days before Kitty left, so that Kitty could show her the house and tell her, on the spot, what had to be done.

When Lizzie arrived and started work, Berridge was inclined to agree with Edith about the prospects for the future. Lizzie Siddle was as brisk and business-like as Kitty. There, however, the resemblance ceased. Lizzie had none of Kitty's grace and charm. She was a striding sort of woman. One could not possibly imagine her playing the coquette with a man.

Berridge agreed to buy Kitty's furniture. Apart from a few personal articles, she didn't want to be bothered with it.

'Have you got a new situation yet?' he ventured.

'Not yet. I shall treat myself to a rest for a while.'

'Have you given Mrs. Berridge a forwarding address?'

'No. But you can always get in touch with me at the Old Swan, Swan Lane, Upper Thames Street. They know me there.'

He made a note of the address. 'I'm sorry you're going, Kitty,' he said.

'I'm sorry to be going myself in a way. But it's for the best, I reckon. Lizzie'll look after you. She'll be happy here, I'm sure. It'll be like a home to Lizzie. She and Missus'll get on like a house afire.'

When it came to the point, Kitty left some hours earlier than she had intended. Berridge was out at the time and so he did not say good-bye to her. On the whole he was relieved.

2

Life at Cassilis Street went on unexpectedly smoothly without Kitty.

Edith managed the lettings pretty well, doing what was necessary, even to the point of saying 'No' quite firmly when some pitiful but obviously undesirable applicant appeared at the front door.

Nothing was heard from Kitty. Sometimes Berridge wondered what she was doing now and whether she had gone up or come down in the world. But for days on end he did not think of her at all.

As for Stephen, even the Sainsburys gave up asking how he liked his new employment. Edith, reading a newspaper by the fire in the evening, would often let her eyes wander from the print to the glowing coals, and one could guess that in all probability she was thinking of Stephen. But she rarely mentioned him now.

Ruth had presented a problem where Stephen was concerned. The girl could hardly be expected to believe that her brother had a position in Paris or anywhere else abroad when she knew perfectly well that no letters came from him. That pretence, in the case of a daughter living at home, could not be kept up for more than a few weeks at the outside. After several bedroom discussions it was decided that Edith should tell Ruth the story about the debt of honour. After all, it might very well be the truth. Certainly Edith appeared to believe it herself.

'Ruth took it more calmly than I should have done in her place,' Edith told her husband afterwards. 'In fact she said that she had always felt that there was something peculiar about Stephen going off suddenly like that. She didn't cry or even seem very upset.'

'Ruth is a bluestocking,' Berridge said. 'Books seem to mean more to her than people.'

By the time Kitty left, the smell hanging about the area had practically gone. Berridge was pleased that after all there need be no taking up of the drains. Possibly it had not been the drains. But whatever it was, it had gone. Lizzie Siddle did on one occasion fancy that she sniffed something. But in view of Lizzie's habit of sniffing, nobody took any notice.

The days passed monotonously and not unpleasantly. After the trouble about Stephen, it was comfortable to sink back into a routine without crises.

Christmas came and went, but the new year proved to be as agreeably uneventful as the last six months of the old year had been. The business in Tottenham Court Road jogged along well enough, and the house was a steady source of income. It had a certain reputation now for clean, quiet, inexpensive lodgings.

The new year was nearing its end when Miss Jane Addington rang the front door bell. It was a bright November morning. Edith was out, and Ruth was at school. Berridge, who had a bad cold, had not gone to business that day.

He was cosseting himself by a fire when Lizzie knocked.

'Two ladies at the front door, sir,' she said. 'Missus is out.'

'What do they want, Lizzie?'

'Two rooms, sir.'

'Are there two vacant?'

'Those that Mr. and Mrs. Greenfield had are ready now.'

The Greenfields had left the week before. They had been good tenants, staid and colourless.

'Ask the ladies to come in, Lizzie,' he said, 'and show them the rooms . . . Oh, by the way, they are quite respectable, are they?'

'Perfectly, sir, I should think.'

Lizzie had kept to her original resolution to have nothing to do with letting the rooms or collecting the lodgers' rents. But she was prepared to show people round, when asked to do so by her employers.

'If they want to take the rooms,' she added, 'shall I bring them in here to see you, sir?'

'Yes, I will see them if Mrs. Berridge has not come back by then.'

Lizzie went off. Berridge hoped that Edith would be back before he had to see the two ladies. But when Lizzie knocked again, Edith was still out.

Two middle-aged females came in with Lizzie, who held the door for them and then departed to continue her normal duties. Berridge rose from his chair.

'We like the rooms,' said the elder lady, 'but there are several points that we wish to discuss before coming to a decision.'

'I am sorry,' he said, 'that my wife, who usually deals with these matters, is out at the moment. Perhaps I can help you.'

'Perhaps so. What is the rent of the rooms?'

The elder lady, who took the lead, was apparently a

Miss Addington. The younger one was her sister Catherine. The lips of both were somewhat drawn down at the corners, the mark of the resigned spinster, Berridge had always understood. Miss Addington, whom her sister addressed as Jane, kept her eyes lowered for much of the time, but Catherine looked at him with interest and even smiled occasionally.

'Now as to coals,' Miss Addington said, when the rent and other matters had been discussed.

'I order the coals,' Berridge told her. 'The lodgers buy what they require from the general stock.'

'I do not like that arrangement. If we take the rooms, we shall order our own coals. I propose to order a ton towards the winter supply. Have you a separate cellar?'

'I have, but it's full of rubbish at present.'

'It could be cleared, could it not?' Miss Addington's tone was peevish, even vaguely offensive. 'I could quite easily get a man to come and clear it.'

'That would not be necessary. I will get it cleared for you.'

'Very well.'

Miss Catherine contrived to send him, with her mild, domestic eyes, the conciliatory message that Jane was not really so much of a dragon as she seemed.

'I will have it done as soon as the tenancy is settled,' he promised.

At that moment Edith returned and took the ladies off. He was not sure whether he wanted them in the house. Catherine would be no trouble at all. But Jane would probably always be displeased about something or other. So far as the coals were concerned, this presented no great difficulty. It would, in fact, provide a good reason for getting rid of the rubbish in the second cellar at last. He would send a boy along from Tottenham Court Road to do the job.

Presently Edith came back.

'Have you let the rooms?' he asked her.

'Yes. The ladies have gone. I think that they will prove to be quite desirable tenants.'

'I didn't take to the elder one. She was too full of what she liked and what she didn't like.'

'Oh, I don't think she will be too bad, John. And Miss Catherine is most pleasant.'

'Yes, she is softer. But very much under her sister's thumb.'

'Well, I expect we shall get used to Miss Jane. They will be coming in a week's time. And they tell me that you are going to clear out the second cellar for their coals.'

'I told them that I would, though I really don't know why they can't do the same as the other tenants about coals.'

'Perhaps after a while they will, dear . . . How does your cold feel now?'

The cold felt better, he told Edith. 'I'll send young Baxter along tomorrow to make a start on the cellar,' he said.

Every now and then during the day he found himself thinking of Miss Catherine's wistful face. A nice woman, that. A pity she was not coming without the sister. Up to the present he had never drifted into a sentimental relationship with any of the female lodgers who from time to time had lived in his house. But that was possibly because none of them had stirred him in that way.

At breakfast next morning Edith said: 'You won't forget to send the boy along to clear the cellar, will you, John?'

'I have made a note to attend to it.'

'Will he be able to finish it in one day, do you suppose?'

'I'll give him a hand-cart. Two or three journeys to Tottenham Court Road ought to be enough. I intend to have the stuff taken to the yard behind the shop and disposed of with some worn-out old rubbish that has been taking up space in the stock-rooms for years.'

'Young Baxter is a good worker, isn't he?' Edith said.

'Yes. A good lad. Only twelve but as hardy as some fellows twice his age. He had been selling boxes of lucifers on the streets for a living when he came to me.'

At the shop that morning Berridge gave the boy his instructions. Young Baxter's coat was torn but it was good enough for the work he had to do. One day in the near future, Berridge promised himself, he would give Baxter some new clothes. Or at any rate some good second-hand clothes.

The lad went off up the street with the hand-cart. An hour later, Berridge was in the shop with a customer who was trying to make up his mind whether or not to buy an eighteenth-century snuff-box. Although the trade done at the shop was mainly in furniture, there was also a certain amount of business in small articles of virtu.

The customer was still hesitating when Baxter reappeared. Berridge frowned as he watched the boy running across the street towards the shop. Baxter ought to have been trudging along with the hand-cart, not running without it.

The lad dived into the side entrance and Berridge lost sight of him. But a moment later there was a slight noise as of someone coming in at the back of the shop. Baxter in his torn coat was standing there, nervously turning his cap round in his hands.

Berridge asked the customer to excuse him and marched over to Baxter. He was annoyed with the customer for wasting time and with Baxter for not being where he was supposed to be.

'What are you doing here, Baxter?' he demanded in an irritable undertone. 'What is the matter? Where is the hand-cart?'

The boy was obviously in a state of intense excitement.

'Please, Mr. Berridge, sir, I had to see you at once. Missus send me. She tell me to run quickly, sir. She want you to come back with me at once.'

'But what is the matter?'

'It's the skeleton,' Baxter whispered. 'In the cellar I come on a bone. And then I find the rest of it, see? Under the old floor-cloth and everything, sir. A 'uman skeleton.'

'Nonsense, boy. You don't know what you're talking about.' It was all too fantastic for words. 'Tell Mrs. Berridge that I will come as soon as possible. And leave everything alone until I get there.'

When young Baxter had gone running off, Berridge went back to the customer.

'I am sorry,' he said, 'but I fear that I shall have to leave you with my shopman. I have had bad news from home.'

The customer was sympathetic. But he would not, he thought, make a decision about the snuff-box that morning.

Berridge summoned his shopman.

'I have to go home for an hour,' he said. 'Look after things, please.'

'Certainly, sir. Nothing wrong, I hope?'

'I don't know yet. Baxter says he has found a skeleton in one of my cellars.'

The shopman gaped. 'A skeleton of a person, sir? A human being, I mean?'

'He seemed to think so.'

Berridge hurried off. If there were in fact human remains in that second cellar, they must have been there since the previous tenant's time. Doubtless the skeleton would prove to be no more than a hospital school specimen that had been discarded, possibly years ago. All the same the previous tenant ought not to have left it in the cellar. Some people really had no sense of the fitness of things.

3

Edith was waiting by the front door.

'I am so thankful that you have come, John.'

'Have you seen this—this thing?'

'No, I haven't. The boy spoke to Lizzie and she came to me at once. But I couldn't bring myself to go in.'

'Where is Baxter now? I told him to leave everything alone until I arrived.'

'He is in the kitchen, I think. Poor boy, he was so upset.'

Berridge went down to the kitchen. In his opinion the boy was not in the least upset. In fact he was probably not likely to enjoy himself so much again for many a year. Not every boy has the good fortune to discover a human skeleton in a neglected cellar.

Young Baxter was eager to go back to his task.

'There might be another, sir,' he suggested.

'Then the police will have to find it. One is enough for me.'

'Yes, sir. Can I come in with you?'

'If you like.'

They went in together through the cellar door, Berridge holding the lamp that the boy had been given when he started work, so that he could see what he was doing. The results of Baxter's labours were evident in a neat pile of rubbish stacked up in one corner ready to be carried out to the handcart.

'There it is, sir,' Baxter muttered. 'Over there, see? There seem to be old floor-cloth wrapped round it. When I pick up the floor-cloth a bone shows at one end. And then I find the rest of it. It slip out almost at me feet, it did . . . See that cord round the neck, sir? Didn't notice that meself, not before this minute.'

Berridge, lamp in hand, bent over the poor huddled bones. Yes, the boy was right. There was a cord round the neck. And it was possible to distinguish fragments that might once have been clothing.

Young Baxter had sharp eyes. 'See that hair, sir, behind the skull?'

Berridge grunted. At forty-nine his eyes were not as sharp as Baxter's. But he could detect the hair. This was no hospital school specimen.

He straightened up. 'Do you know where the police station is?'

'Yes, sir.'

'Run along right away. Give them the address and ask them to send a constable. Bring one back with you if you can.'

After the boy had gone Berridge told himself that he ought to have gone to the station personally. He would have got more attention than that youngster. But the prospect of walking into a police station with an unlikely story about a skeleton was more than, at that moment, he could face.

He went indoors to get away from the revolting cellar, washed his face and hands and drank a little brandy . . . Those damned Addington women and their damned coals! Why in Heaven's name did they have to come to Cassilis Street looking for rooms?

After the brandy he felt calmer. Whoever was responsible for those remains, he wasn't. His mistake had lain in not clearing out the cellar as soon as they moved in, more than two and a half years ago.

Edith was hovering near him anxiously. 'Who knows about this?' he asked her.

'Only Lizzie, I think, apart from ourselves and the boy. I fancy that not even Nelly knows, but I couldn't be sure.'

'The lodgers don't know?'

'Not yet.'

Strange that only a few hours ago he had been half looking forward to a pleasantly sentimental relationship with Miss Catherine Addington. Life had become so peaceful that the promise of even such a tenuous affair as this had been mildly titillating. Yet it had been so completely driven from his mind now that he didn't care if he never saw her again. He doubted, in point of fact, whether in any event he ever would see either of the Addington sisters again. When she got to hear about the skeleton, Miss Jane would certainly not wish to take those two rooms.

Young Baxter came back with a constable, and Berridge took the man into the cellar.

The constable peered at the bones. 'How long have you lived here, sir?' he enquired.

'Just over two and a half years. The remains must have been here when we took the house. There was a pile of rubbish in here that the previous tenant left.'

'And you never had it cleared out till today?'

'No. We didn't use the cellar. The job was put off.'

'What made you do it today, sir?'

Berridge told the constable about the Misses Addington and their coals. He foresaw that he would have to explain the matter many times to different people in the near future, and his heart sank.

The constable departed to fetch a sergeant. 'Keep the cellar locked, please, sir,' he said before he left. 'Nobody must go in.'

The constable was soon back, and a sergeant was with him. They were both in the cellar for about twenty minutes. When they came out, the sergeant said: 'A nasty business, sir.'

Berridge told his story over again.

'I can't understand,' said the sergeant, 'how she can have been there all that time, and nobody aware of it.'

'She?'

'Oh, yes, it is obviously a woman's skeleton, sir.' The sergeant pulled out his watch. 'When can you call at the station, Mr. Berridge?' he asked.

'It is getting on for dinner-time now. What about half past two?'

'Very good, sir.'

It was only then that Berridge realised that he might conceivably be charged with murder. Until then he had been aware of nothing more than indignation and self-criticism.

He had been angry with the previous tenant, annoyed with himself. But something in the sergeant's tone sent a thrill of fear through him.

Dinner was a silent meal. He ate it absent-mindedly. Edith and Ruth both looked shocked and worried. Edith had told Ruth as soon as she came in from school. There was no point in keeping it from her, as she was bound to know soon in any case. And whoever was guilty, it couldn't be any member of the Berridge family.

At the police station that afternoon it seemed to Berridge that for the moment they only wanted to know certain quite ordinary facts about him. His full name, the date and place of his birth, his previous addresses, his wife's maiden name, the number and sex and ages of his children: all these and sundry other details were noted down. The Inspector who interviewed him was polite and business-like.

As Berridge was going the Inspector said: 'I understand that Inspector Vickery is to be placed in charge of the case. He will no doubt be calling upon you.'

Inspector Vickery called at Cassilis Street shortly after breakfast on the following morning. He proved to be a heavy, middle-aged man with lazy eyes and a slow, quiet way of speaking. Edith remarked afterwards that he had an extremely pleasant smile and was not in the least like her idea of a police officer.

At first he spent most of his time in the cellar. Constables arrived and the skeleton was taken away. Lights were brought in, lights much brighter than the lamp by which the boy Baxter had worked. The contents of the cellar were no doubt being gone through systematically for evidence of the identity of the woman to whom the bones and the hair and the scraps of clothing had belonged.

For the police did not know who the woman might have been. And nobody in the house could tell them.

'The doctors, Mr. Berridge,' said Inspector Vickery, when he came again next day, 'think that the remains may have been in the cellar for about two years. The woman may have died from a blow on the back of the head. The skull showed marks of violence. But there was also that cord round the neck, suggesting strangulation. The age of the woman is not certain, but she wasn't a young girl. She wasn't a big woman. And it seems likely that the hair was worn in short curls or ringlets. It may have been dyed. It is possible that the woman suffered from a slight curvature of the spine.'

The Inspector was seated comfortably in an easy chair in the private parlour at Cassilis Street. Edith was there too, looking white and tired. Berridge tried to concentrate on what the Inspector had just said.

'I am sure,' he replied at last, 'that no woman disappeared from this house since we came here. All sorts of casual lodgers left after a short stay, but we always knew about it.'

'Nobody vanished without paying?'

'Nobody. We have been lucky in that respect.'

The Inspector moved on to another point. 'Was the door from the area to the cellar kept locked? At night, for instance?'

'It should have been locked at night. But there may have been nights when it was left unlocked. It would have been quite possible, I suppose, if the door was unlocked, for a stranger to come down the area steps from the street in the dark, put the body in the cellar and make off again.'

'It is possible, I agree. I had thought of it myself.'

'But my own view,' Berridge pressed, 'is still that the remains were there when we took the house.'

The Inspector turned to Edith. 'If you will excuse my mentioning the matter, Mrs. Berridge, did you not at any time notice an unpleasant smell coming from the cellars.'

Edith glanced at Berridge and he answered for her. 'There was a smell,' he said, 'but it passed off.'

'We thought it was the drains,' Edith said.

'And when,' the Inspector enquired, 'did you notice this smell?'

They both considered. 'During the spring of last year, we first noticed it,' Edith said. And then, in her simple way, she added: 'I remember that, because it was soon after Stephen left us.'

Berridge was conscious of a sort of hardening in Inspector Vickery's lazy eyes.

'Stephen? Your son, Mrs. Berridge?'

'Well, my husband's son actually. I am his stepmother.'

'And Stephen left the house during the spring of last year, did he? Where is he now?'

'We don't know, Inspector.' She seemed to be suddenly on the edge of tears. 'It is a sad story, I am afraid.'

Berridge cleared his throat. 'My son deceived us,' he said stiffly, 'for reasons that we were never fully aware of.'

The Inspector was interested. 'I am afraid that I must ask you to tell me about this deception. It may have been quite unconnected with the case. But you will appreciate that I ought to know about it.'

Berridge stared at a picture on the wall opposite. 'It is,' he began, 'as Mrs. Berridge says, a sad story. I hoped that I should never have to refer to it again. But if I must, here it is, so far as I remember it.'

The Inspector listened and nodded and asked a few questions. Edith broke into the narrative to correct her husband on one or two points.

'Very mysterious,' said Inspector Vickery, when Berridge had finished. He sounded impressed. The story, it appeared, had carried conviction.

'This housemaid or housekeeper or whatever she was,' the Inspector added, 'this Kitty Daniels . . . It is not possible, I suppose, that the remains in the cellar may be hers?'

Berridge involuntarily winced. 'Quite impossible, I should say. She was a tall well-built woman.'

'How old was she when she left?'

'About thirty.'

'And you did not hear from her again?'

'No. We parted on perfectly good terms. In fact we should have liked her to stay. But she didn't get in touch with us after she went and we don't know where she is.'

The Inspector crossed his legs and looked as cosy as though he might be proposing to sit in the easy chair for the rest of the day. But a few minutes later he glanced at the clock on the mantelpiece and said: 'Goodness, is that the time? I must be going.'

Smiling his pleasant smile he went down the steps from the front door.

When he was gone, Berridge said: 'He suspects Stephen.'

Edith, back in the parlour, sank wearily into the chair lately vacated by the Inspector. 'If he does,' she replied, 'he must be a very foolish man.'

'He isn't a fool, my dear.'

'No, I know he isn't really, John. But it is too absurd to suppose that Stephen had anything to do with it. Or Kitty either for that matter.'

Berridge didn't press the point. He clung to his view that the remains in the cellar went back to the time of the previous tenant. One had to admit, of course, that that smell had been peculiar. The smell had started, as Edith had told the Inspector, at about the time of Stephen's disappearance. But that must have been mere coincidence.

In any case, who the devil was the woman in the cellar?

He felt as if a malicious spirit of evil had taken possession of his house, plunging it into a state of bewildering unreason. And there was nothing that he could do. Except answer questions.

4

Newspapers and reporters; policemen and detectives coming and going; people loitering outside the house, gaping stupidly at it: Berridge put up with them all, suffering them with as much cheerfulness as he could command.

The rumours were less easy to endure. He was made aware that stories were going about and that in Cassilis Street his arrest was regarded as imminent. Other bodies had been found, it was alleged, in the cellars and elsewhere. One day he even had to get police protection as he went out, because of the menacing attitude of a group of rough characters waiting for him on the pavement.

But the important thing was that the police did not appear to suspect him. Nor, it seemed, did they suspect Edith.

'They pretty evidently take the view,' he told Edith, 'that if we had known what was in that cellar we shouldn't have let Baxter clear the place out. We should have done it ourselves and disposed of the remains quietly somehow or other.'

'We haven't heard anything further from those Miss Addingtons,' she remarked.

'I don't suppose we shall.'

'The regular lodgers have been very good. Not one has given notice so far. They are just staying on as though nothing had happened.'

The rooms that the Addington sisters were to have had were still vacant. The regulars might be firm enough, but there had been no people at the front door asking for lodgings since the news of the murder had appeared in the papers.

Murder it certainly was, according to the police.

'When I walk away from the house,' Berridge said to Edith, 'I can feel eyes boring into my back.'

'Nonsense, dear. You are fancying things.'

'I don't think so. I shall dread going to chapel next Sunday.'

'Then I shall go alone, John.'

Her courage was admirable. Edith, for all her palpitations, had stood up well to the shock, once she had got used to it.

Berridge's business in Tottenham Court Road was not much affected. Customers and employees occasionally looked at him as they would not have done before. But in the main the business went on as usual.

And the servants at Cassilis Street stayed at their posts.

Lizzie Siddle took the murder in her long stride. It was no concern of hers, her manner suggested, if a skeleton had been found on the premises. If she had had her way, of course, the cellar would have been cleared out months before. There was never any question of her leaving. She liked her situation far too much to give it up. At Cassilis Street there was no condescending lady's maid to patronise her, no master who swore at the footmen, no footmen to get in her way. She was addressed as Lizzie, never as Siddle, and she liked that more than anything. All this she had confided to Edith at odd times. She was not a talker, but there were moments when she was moved to lift the veil that concealed her sentiments from the world. It was, however, only for Edith that the veil was lifted. To Edith's husband she had little to say. What she did in her spare time, when she took her bedroom candlestick and went upstairs to the attic floor, nobody ever knew. Probably, Berridge supposed, she merely undressed, got into bed and slept, for she was always about by six o'clock in the morning.

Lizzie might have no interest in the murder, but Lizzie's underling had a great deal. Nelly was prepared to discuss it with all and sundry, and she gloried in the celebrity that the affair conferred upon her in the eyes of her friends.

Inspector Vickery approved of Nelly. 'I got more from Nelly Cloke than I did from all the other occupants of the house put together,' he told Berridge. 'Except,' he added politely, 'yourself and Mrs. Berridge.'

Berridge was momentarily puzzled. 'Nelly Cloke?'

'Yes. The general.'

'Oh yes, of course. You mean Nelly. I am sorry, Inspector. I had forgotten that she had a surname.'

'Well, she has, apparently. And she has another thing too. A good memory. You will recollect that I went through the rent book with Mrs. Berridge and yourself, but neither of you could remember much about many of the casual lodgers. Now Nelly seems to remember them all, and I came to the conclusion, from what she told me, that there were several cases that seemed worth investigating.'

Berridge said coldly that he was pleased that Nelly had been of some assistance. 'But I should not place too much reliance on what she says. I need not tell you what the minds of young females of that sort are like. You will know quite as well as I do. It is natural, I suppose, that she would remember the lodgers better than Mrs. Berridge or myself would do. Nelly saw them frequently in the course of her work. But until Kitty Daniels left, my wife and I had very little to do with the lodgers.'

The Inspector said that he understood the position. 'When Kitty Daniels left,' he added, 'didn't she give you a forwarding address?'

'She did, as a matter of fact.' Berridge felt in his pocket for his notebook. 'Here it is . . . The Old Swan, Swan Lane, Upper Thames Street. She said, I fancy, that I could get in touch with her there. But I never had occasion to do so.'

The Inspector made a note. 'One of my young fellows can go along there and make some enquiries.'

So far as Berridge was aware, the police were at a dead end. They might, after the manner of policemen, know more than they told. But he surmised that they knew very little more now than when Inspector Vickery had been placed in charge of the case. They didn't know, for instance, when or how the victim had been killed. It might have been about two years ago. And it might have been either by a blow or by strangling. All very vague, especially as they didn't even know who the victim was. They suspected that Kitty was concerned. And also Stephen. But that was only because Stephen had disappeared in mysterious circumstances, and

Kitty had thrown up a good situation for no very satisfactory reason. There was nothing definite, Berridge was certain, to connect either of them with the murder.

Inspector Vickery came and went in his rather casual way. He had decided to go to the Old Swan himself, Berridge was informed, but the publican who had been there when Kitty had given the address was dead now and the widow had moved away. Eventually the Inspector had got hold of a potman who was acquainted with Kitty Daniels. This potman had heard that Kitty had fallen on evil times. He had even been told that she was in the Westminster House of Correction at the moment, serving a prison sentence for a petty theft.

'It may be completely untrue,' the Inspector said. 'In any case it is easily checked. I only had the talk with the potman this morning. He was away when I first called at the Swan, and the publican pretended that he didn't know where the man was. People never know anything when the police want information. However, I tried again today and saw the fellow. I am inclined to think that he knew what he was talking about. Anyhow I sent one of my men along to Westminster straight away because I wanted to come here myself and have another talk with Nelly Cloke. As a matter of fact I have just been talking to her.'

They were in the private parlour again, Berridge and Edith and the Inspector. Berridge had been reading and Edith was sewing. It was a shock to Berridge to learn—assuming that the potman's story was true—that Kitty was in prison.

He found it hard to believe. He had had a high opinion of the police, but their handling of this case did not impress him favourably. Inspector Vickery himself was a pleasant enough man. He certainly didn't keep one in the dark about things. But on the other hand he didn't seem to be very sharp. If, for example, Kitty was known to the police, the Inspector ought surely to have been aware of this days ago, without waiting to be informed of it by a potman.

Inspector Vickery stroked his jowl and repeated: 'Yes, I have been talking to your Nelly Cloke again. You remember that I went through the rent book with Nelly and she was very helpful. As I think I told you, there were several cases that struck me as being worth investigation . . . Well, they have been investigated. There were three such cases, and in two of them the ladies in question were traced and proved to be alive and well. The remaining case produced no results at all.' His eyes rested for a moment on Berridge and then moved across to Edith. 'Do you, either of you, remember a Miss Fairford?'

Berridge replied at once that he did. 'She was an elderly spinster, an odd person who tried to behave like a young woman. I only remember her, in fact, because she was so eccentric.'

'It was rather sad,' Edith remarked, 'to see a woman of her age conducting herself so unsuitably.'

'Miss Fairford was only here for a few weeks, I believe,' Berridge said. 'We were rather glad when she left because she used to spy on the other lodgers. There were several complaints, I fancy.'

Edith dropped her sewing. 'Kitty used to say that Miss Fairford was always talking about Bath, where she had lived for many years. She talked to Kitty chiefly, and Kitty used to tell me.'

Berridge shifted uneasily in his chair. 'You surely aren't suggesting that Miss Fairford . . .'

He couldn't bring himself to finish the sentence.

'I am not suggesting anything yet,' said the Inspector. 'It is just a line of enquiry. Can you recollect the circumstances in which Miss Fairford left the house?'

Berridge looked at Edith. 'Do you remember anything special, my dear?'

Edith closed her eyes for a moment of concentration. 'I

seem to recollect,' she said at last, 'Kitty telling me that Miss Fairford had left somewhat suddenly. But I couldn't be absolutely sure of that. I am not even certain, Mr. Inspector, that I was here at the time. I spend a few days at Windsor now and then, you see, with my aunt, who is getting on in years. You will understand that in a house like this, people come and go. And at that time I had nothing to do with the lodgers. Kitty did it all.'

Berridge said that he remembered Kitty telling him that Miss Fairford had left. 'But as Mrs. Berridge says, the casual lodgers are always coming and going, and Miss Fairford's departure made no particular impression on me. Except, as I said just now, that I do remember feeling relieved that she had gone, for the reason that I mentioned to you.'

'Were you aware that Miss Fairford sometimes went under the name of Falkland?'

'I don't think so. She was always known as Miss Fairford here.'

Edith couldn't recall having heard anything of the sort either. But it had all happened nearly two years ago. 'And really,' she concluded plaintively, 'I have hardly given poor Miss Fairford a thought since she went.'

'Kitty Daniels,' Berridge said, 'is the only one who might help you.'

He was tired of the questioning. Besides, he didn't believe that the skeleton in the cellar had been Miss Fairford's. Inspector Vickery was wasting his time. He was on the wrong tack. The previous tenant of the house was the man that he ought to be badgering.

There was a tap at the door. It was Lizzie. 'A police officer to speak to the Inspector,' she announced with a sniff.

Inspector Vickery went off to speak to the officer privately.

Berridge yawned wearily. 'That fellow will never catch the criminal,' he grumbled to Edith. 'All this fuss about Miss Fairford!' Sitting there, waiting for the Inspector to come back, he found himself longing inexpressibly for the return of the peaceful jog-trot of the time between Kitty's going and the discovery of the skeleton.

The door clicked slightly and the Inspector strolled in.

'The potman was right,' he said. 'Kitty Daniels is in the Westminster House of Correction.'

He wouldn't stay any longer today, he added. He proposed to go along to Westminster at once and see Kitty Daniels for himself.

6

I

INSPECTOR VICKERY was a Somerset man, the fifth son of a struggling farmer in the rough country of the Brendon Hills. There was no future for him on the farm, and at first he had thought of enlisting as a soldier, but somebody had suggested the new Metropolitan Police Force. The money for the journey was found and before long, somewhat to his own surprise, young James Vickery was a constable in London.

He made a good police officer and promotion came his way pretty easily. He missed the fresh air of the fields. But there were compensations. For the first time in his life he had money of his own. Not much, but enough to make him feel independent. And now that he was an Inspector he had as much money as he wanted, a well-dressed wife and a nice house in Kentish Town.

At the Westminster House of Correction Inspector Vickery was well known, and when he asked to see Mr. Eccles he was taken at once to a room at the end of a long passage. Eccles, a solid man with an air of great respectability, was working on some papers that were spread out on the table before him. Vickery lowered his bulk into a chair and crossed his legs.

'What have you got there?' he asked, faintly curious.

'Tenders for supplying the prison with meat, oatmeal, rice, treacle and soap. We feed well here.'

'And keep clean apparently.'

'Oh yes, we see to it that they wash themselves . . . I suppose you want to see Martha Daniels.'

'Kitty Daniels,' Vickery said.

'That's what she calls herself. Martha is her name.'

'What is she in for?'

'Stealing a trinket. Nothing much. Never done such a thing before, so far as is known. Anyhow, she never got caught before.'

'What is she like?'

'Docile sort of woman. No trouble at all. Not bad-looking. What have you got against her?'

'I don't know yet. Can I see her now?'

'Any time you like. See her in this room if you like. I'll just take these tenders away. I can get on with them somewhere else.'

He gathered his papers together and went off. Vickery sat and waited, thinking in a desultory way about the case. He had recently seen the two spinster sisters whose demand for a separate cellar at Cassilis Street had set things going. The elder Miss Addington's indignation at being involved in a murder case was a spectacle to remember. But they had satisfied him that Berridge's tale about the cellar was true.

He felt sure that Berridge had had nothing to do with the murder, and even more certain that Mrs. Berridge knew nothing about it. Neither of them was of the stuff of which good liars are made and Berridge obviously believed his own story that the skeleton must have been in the cellar when he took the house.

The doctors had considered this and had thought it unlikely. Also there was the matter of the smell, that could not possibly be left out of account.

The floor-cloth that had been rolled round the body had yielded no clues. Time and damp had obliterated every trace of a pattern, and it almost fell to pieces when it was taken out of the cellar.

Vickery had found the previous tenant of the house and questioned him at the Opera House in Covent Garden, where the man had a situation as an assistant manager. He proved to be a lordly individual who had been living beyond his means and had matrimonial troubles into the bargain. In spite of these untoward circumstances, however, Vickery was convinced that the man was harmless enough. He didn't even seem to know that there were two cellars at the Cassilis Street house, and he remembered nothing about any pile of rubbish.

They seemed to be a long time bringing that woman Daniels in. Nelly Cloke at Cassilis Street had hinted that Kitty Daniels was no better than she should be. Nelly had evidently been afraid of Kitty Daniels and jealous of her superior charms. Kitty had been much too friendly with Mr. Berridge, in Nelly's considered opinion. And too friendly with young Mr. Stephen as well. It was a funny business, Nelly had whispered. Carrying on with the father and the son at the same time. 'It wasn't safe to go into her room without knocking and waiting for an answer, I can tell you, mister.' The carrying on with the son, Vickery inferred from Nelly's confused narrative, had been fairly open and above board. On the other hand, the carrying on with the father had been on the sly.

The regular lodgers were unhelpful. They were not actually obstructive but they didn't wish to be mixed up in the case. They had good lodgings, cheap and comfortable for that part of London, and they clearly wanted things to continue at Cassilis Street as they had always been. They weren't going to say a word against Berridge or his wife. As regards Kitty Daniels they had evidently liked her and had been sorry when she left. Not one of them had any suggestion to make about the identity of the murdered woman. Several remembered the smell but they had not thought much about it at the time.

'London,' the young fellow from the north called Walker

had said, 'is a smelly place. One smell more or less makes no difference. Happen you've never been to Lancashire, Inspector. If you have you will no doubt agree with me that in spite of the mills the place is cleaner than London. It's the people, you see. Right clean, hard-working people up there, all of them.'

Vickery had a talk with Ruth Berridge, the daughter. The girl had led a sheltered life and wasn't likely to know of anything sordid that might have been going on under her parents' roof. He did question her about Stephen, the half-brother, however. Had she received a letter or a message from Stephen?

'Nothing at all.' She was nervous but not evasive. 'If I had, I should have told my mother and father about it.'

'Even though Stephen had asked you not to?'

'Yes. I think so. But in any case if he had written to me here, Dad would have seen the letter when it arrived and would have recognised the handwriting.'

'Stephen could surely have written to you care of the school where you are employed.'

'I never receive letters of any sort addressed to the school. Miss Picknett would not like it.'

'Why do you think he went away?'

'He had to leave the country because of a gambling debt.'

'How do you know that, Miss Berridge?'

'Mother told me.'

'What did Stephen do in the evenings?' he asked.

'When he was at home, do you mean? He played the piano mostly.'

'And when he was not at home?'

'I have no notion.'

'Didn't he talk to you about the places he went to and the people he was with?'

'Never.'

'Never about his women friends?'

'No. I didn't know that he had any. Except Kitty, and we didn't take that seriously.'

That was about all he got from Ruth Berridge. Vickery had seen Stephen's music-room, which was kept, he was told, just as it had been when Stephen had used it, on the apparent assumption that Stephen might come back at any time. There wasn't much furniture in it—the piano, a music stool, a heavy fender, a couple of chairs, not much else.

Nelly Cloke had no doubts about the case. She was sure that the skeleton was Miss Fairford's. And also that Kitty Daniels had done for the poor lady.

'I been looking for Miss Fairford,' she confided to Vickery. 'Ever since they found the skeleton I been looking for her. And asking my friends round here too. Nobody has ever set eyes on her since she left. You'd think someone would have seen her or heard of her, wouldn't you, mister? If she was about, you couldn't miss her, got up the way she was. And it isn't likely she would move far from this part of London. It suited her round here, she told me so, see? She'd lodged in several places before she come here. Using different names.'

'What names?' Vickery had asked.

'Falkland was one. She used that name in Mornington Crescent. She didn't tell me that herself though. My friend in Mornington Crescent told me, so I know it's true.'

Vickery fished out the notebook that he carried in his waistcoat pocket.

'What number in Mornington Crescent?' he said. Nelly told him. 'And there's another thing you ought to know, mister.' She lowered her voice. 'After Miss Fairford was supposed to have left, I was doing the floor in Kitty Daniels' room one day and noticed a watch and chain that I had seen Miss Fairford wearing. I know that because Miss Fairford showed it to me once and on the back it had "Delia Faber, Bath, 1840". I can see it as clear as if it was yesterday, though

I haven't said a word about it to a living soul before this moment, mister.'

Vickery tapped on the notebook with his pencil. 'Miss Fairford may have given Kitty the watch and chain,' he remarked.

'Not she. I didn't dislike the old party, but she was mean as muck, and nobody as knew her could say different. She wouldn't give away any watch and chain to Kitty or anybody else. No, mister, Kitty got hold of that watch and chain somehow, and how she did it we don't know though we may guess. She wouldn't have sent me up to clean her floor if she'd remembered that she left that watch lying around Besides, Kitty wasn't exactly a favourite with Miss Fairford. I heard them once going at it hammer and tongs. At least Kitty was. She was telling Miss Fairford that if she went round the house spying on people she'd have to leave. And Miss Fairford was pleading to be allowed to stay. I happened to be outside the door, doing the landing, see?'

'Miss Fairford, or whatever she was called, came from Bath, did she?'

'Oh yes, sir, everybody knew that. She told me some queer stories when I was doing her room. Shocking, some of 'em!'

Nelly went on to talk about Stephen. It was evident that she had adored him from afar. But Vickery was less interested now in Stephen Berridge. More and more plainly the finger pointed to Kitty Daniels.

Sitting in Mr. Eccles' room at the Westminster House of Correction Vickery pondered these matters. Where there had been, a few days ago, almost nothing to work on, a pattern was beginning to emerge.

At last, the sound of footsteps in the passage indicated that Kitty Daniels was probably coming. About time too. He had been waiting long enough.

A wardress knocked and entered, with a tallish woman in prison clothes.

'I'll be outside, sir,' said the wardress, 'in case you want me.'

Vickery rose and motioned the woman to a chair. He was always courteous to women, whoever they were. It was something that his mother had taught him long ago, and the habit of courtesy remained.

2

Kitty Daniels sat down. She was a woman who must have been worth looking at in her youth, Vickery thought. The remains of beauty were still there, but the marks of dissipation were there too. Her manner was dull and apathetic.

'My name is Vickery,' he said. 'Inspector Vickery. I am investigating the murder at Cassilis Street.'

She nodded carelessly. 'I read about it in the papers. They let us see the papers here.'

'You were a housemaid there, weren't you?'

'Housekeeper,' she corrected him. 'But I left eighteen months ago.'

'Why didn't you tell them here that you had been employed at Cassilis Street?'

'Why should I tell them? The case was nothing to do with me. I left there eighteen months ago.'

Her indifferent tone was like a blank wall. But there was a distinct trace of Somerset in her voice. He was sure of it.

'Do you come from Somerset?' he said.

'I did. What of it?'

'You still have a trace of the Somerset accent. I am a Somerset man myself, you see. From West Somerset. The Brendon Hills, fifteen miles west of Taunton.'

She seemed to soften a little. Yes, she had often heard of Taunton, as a young girl, but she had never been there. 'Our nearest town was Bridgwater. I remember walking to Bridgwater from our village and back again more than once.'

'Do you ever go home to Somerset?'

'No. There's nobody down there belonging to me now.'

'You don't want to go back for the sake of old times?'

'No. I never had any very good times down there.' Then, with a touch of animation that was like sunshine on her face: 'London's been my home for years. London's where I've had my good times.'

'I can say much the same, I suppose.' He pulled out his notebook and prepared to get down to business. 'Now, would you mind telling me what you have been doing since you left Cassilis Street?'

'No. I don't mind. I've been doing myself no good, if you must know. I couldn't seem to find a situation I liked. And I got in with a man that I thought was fond of me, but all he wanted was my money. I had some money when I left Cassilis Street. But this man soon got through it. You know the sort of thing—drinking every night until the money was gone. Gambling too. And that was the end of it. The end of him too, so far as I was concerned.' She stared down at her clasped hands. 'Men are a dirty lot,' she muttered.

'Where were you living with this man?'

'We had a room in Drury Lane.'

'What was his name?'

'I knew him as Charley Owen.'

'What did he do?'

'Nothing. Nothing regular, I mean. He'd been a pickpocket at one time. He wanted me to go with men and give him the money I got. I won't say I haven't obliged a gentleman friend once or twice in my life. But I wouldn't do it for money. It was after we quarrelled about me refusing to go with men that he went off. Stole everything he could lay hands on when he went, the dirty rat did.'

It was an old story, the sort of story that Vickery had listened to many times before. If you were a police officer you saw more of the sordid side of life than most people did. Sometimes Vickery got tired of it, sick and tired and nauseated, and wished that he had stayed in West Somerset and got work as a coachman or something of the kind, living in fresh air among decent people.

'So after that you found yourself another situation, did you?' he prompted her.

'Yes. At a public house. Not good service, but the best I could get then. I had been there two months when this trouble about the brooch happened. It's no good my telling you I didn't take it. It was found in my room and what could I say? Somebody put it there, somebody that didn't like me.'

She talked in the resigned and expressionless style of one who was convinced that, for the time being at least, the tide of life was running against her.

'Why didn't you try to get back your old situation at Cassilis Street?' he said.

'I didn't feel like going back. I don't believe in going back to places. In any case Mrs. Berridge probably wouldn't have wanted me.'

'Why not?'

She took a little time to consider her reply. 'Did you see Lizzie Siddle at Cassilis Street?' she asked at length.

'I did.'

'She took my place, as I suppose you know. She's a first-class servant, well-trained, no nonsense about her. They wouldn't give Lizzie notice to have me back.'

She smiled as she spoke, and again he got the impression of sunshine briefly lighting up her face.

'Do you remember a Miss Fairford who lodged at Cassilis Street?' he demanded abruptly.

'Yes, I remember the old dolly.' The answer came without a trace of evasion. 'She wasn't in the house long. But she caused trouble enough while she was there, spying on the other lodgers. There were some rare scenes, I can tell you. Mr. Berridge was glad when she left and so was I. She was a queer one, she was.'

'When did she leave?'

'I forget. It would be in the rent book, which I dare say you've seen. As far as I recollect it would have been some time in the early spring last year.'

'Did you see her go?'

'I got a cab for her and put her things in it. She didn't have much.'

'What address did she give the cabby?'

'Oh, Lord, I don't know. I may have heard but I don't remember now. I didn't care where she was going as long as she went.'

'Did she leave a forwarding address?'

'I don't think so. But I couldn't be certain.'

'Most lodgers do when they move, don't they?'

'Yes, most of them . . . You're very curious about her, aren't you? Surely you don't think those bones in the cellar were hers? If you do, I should say you were barking up the wrong tree with a vengeance.'

'Whoever it was,' he said, 'didn't crawl into that cellar and die there. The doctors say that the skeleton was that of an elderly woman who had been killed, possibly two years ago or rather less. The descriptions of Miss Fairford that various people have given me suggest that she may have been the victim. It would help me a good deal if you could tell me what you remember of the lady.'

'All right. I don't mind. If it pleases you.'

She sat back in the chair and stared at the wall opposite, as though collecting her thoughts, before she began. Then she told her story quite naturally and straightforwardly. If anything was being suppressed or distorted, he could detect no sign of it.

In general the story agreed with what he had already heard from the Berridges and Nelly Cloke and the lodgers at Cassilis Street. But Kitty Daniels seemed to know more of Miss Fairford's background than the others. As she talked, Vickery found himself being carried along by the tale of the three sisters at Bath, the indulgent father and the youngest daughter Delia, who preferred dalliance to marriage, until at last she got too old for either. Kitty made him see the poor little bedizened scrap of a woman, as Kitty herself had first seen Miss Fairford, on the front steps of the house in Cassilis Street on that cold January morning nearly two years ago. He was held by Kitty's account of the spying from windows, the listening at keyholes, the obsession with other people's lives. It was a sad business. But it didn't seem to lead up to that blow on the skull, that piece of rope round the neck.

'Didn't she have any friends?' he asked.

'None that I ever heard of. She liked to go to Mr. Stephen's music-room and sit there while he played his piano. But you wouldn't call that friendship. He was just being kind to her.'

'You knew Mr. Stephen pretty well, didn't you?'

'He used to take me out in the evening sometimes.'

'Nothing else?'

'No. Nothing else. Who said there was anything else?'

He did not answer the question. 'You were in love with him, weren't you?' he said gently.

She laughed to herself. It was a bitter laugh, that made him feel sorry for her.

'It is stupid,' she said, 'to fall in love with somebody who can never belong to you.'

She had not answered his question. But there was no need to press the point. Young Berridge had apparently disentangled himself when he found that things were going too far, and he had done it in a way that seemed callous to the point of cruelty. Kitty had said that he had been kind to Miss Fairford, and that, of course, might well be true. A man who was kind to an old lady could sometimes be pretty cruel to a younger one.

'What sort of man was Mr. Stephen?' he said.

'To look at, you mean? Rather short and stocky. Always nicely dressed. Took a pride in his appearance. He wanted to get on in the world. I suppose that was the chief thing about him.'

A sombre story, as dark in its different way as Miss Fairford's. Young Berridge, one assumed, had found another woman. Not a housekeeper or a housemaid. More likely a well-to-do widow who had taken him in tow, possibly abroad, as her lover. Or even perhaps as her husband. And Kitty Daniels, not very long after, had thrown herself into the arms of a sneak-thief, drowning her sorrow in drink and gambling and the illusion of Charley Owen's fondness for her. Until at last she had reached the Westminster House of Correction.

'I have been told that Miss Fairford was mean,' Vickery said, putting Stephen Berridge abruptly to one side.

'Who told you that? Nelly Cloke, I suppose, the dirty liar. No, Miss Fairford wasn't mean, whatever else she was. She gave me several things before she went. She wouldn't need them much longer, she said, so I might as well have them.'

'What things?'

'Oh, various things . . . A black lace scarf, a lace collar and some other clothes. And a pair of ear-rings. And a watch and chain that she said an admirer had given her.'

'Have you still got them?'

'Only the watch. I sold the other things.'

'Where is the watch now?'

'I don't know. They took it away when I was put in here.'

Vickery pushed back his chair. It would take a clever barrister to show that Miss Fairford hadn't given Kitty Daniels the watch. Kitty was clever too. She knew that the watch was among her belongings. So she had admitted to it and accounted for it before she was challenged.

'I may be coming to see you again soon,' he said, getting up and going to the door.

'Very good, sir.'

She was subdued and respectful now. The female warder

took her away and Vickery went in search of Mr. Eccles.

'Have you got Martha Daniels' possessions here?' he said, when he found him.

'Not in this room. But I know where I can put my hand on them. Chiefly clothes, as far as I remember, as is usual women are concerned. And a few trinkets and such like.'

'And a watch?'

'Yes, I fancy there was a watch. But it was chiefly clothes.'

'Can we take a look at the watch now?'

'By all means. Come along with me. It was an old watch, I fancy. Or at any rate not in the style of the ladies' watches you see in the shops now. And it had a name on the back. It may have been stolen but nobody at the public house where she worked knew anything about it.'

Eccles' memory was not at fault. The watch was there, and it was obviously the one that Nelly Cloke had seen in Kitty's room. The face bore, in tiny lettering, the name of a Bath watch-maker.

'I should like to take this away with me,' Vickery said.

Mr. Eccles pursed his lips dubiously. 'How long will you want to keep it?'

'I am not sure.'

'Well, I'll trust you with it. She won't be out for two months. Will it be back by then?'

'I hope so.'

'Very well. Give me a receipt. One can't be too careful with prisoners' belongings.' Mr. Eccles lowered his voice importantly. 'Did you get what you wanted from Martha Daniels?'

'I got something.'

'It is the Cassilis Street murder, isn't it?'

'She was there at the time. Assuming that we have the probable date of death right.'

'And what is the next move?'

'I'm going down to Bath this evening.'

'Mr. Eccles looked wise but asked no more questions.

'I've never been to Bath,' he said.

3

James Vickery had never been to Bath before either. In the farm-house on the Brendon Hills, the city of Bath, though in the same county, was no more than a name, a place where well-to-do ladies and gentlemen resided or which they visited to drink the waters. His duties as a police officer had never taken him there before. And it had never occurred to him to spend a holiday there.

It was late when he reached Bath. He found a hotel, had a meal and went to bed. After breakfast next morning he called at the police station. When he left Paddington he had known nothing but the watch-maker's name and the fact that he had been located at Bath twenty-odd years ago. The man might be dead now. But at the police station Vickery was informed that the shop was still in existence.

'And the same man is there,' he was told. 'Mr. Naylor has been there for over forty years. He's getting long in the tooth now but as good as ever at his work, people say. The shop is nothing to look at.'

'Where exactly is the shop?' he asked.

'Lilliput Alley. In the old part of the city.'

A constable was directed to take Inspector Vickery to the watchmaker's and they set off together. In a narrow lane near the Abbey the constable said: 'Here it is, sir.'

'Wait outside at the corner. I don't want to frighten Mr. Naylor.'

A bell jangled excitedly as Vickery pushed open the shop door. Presently an elderly man came in from a room at the back, a dumpy, portly little figure with sad blue eyes. He was lame and, even indoors, walked with the aid of a stick.

Vickery explained who he was and produced the watch.

'You made this, did you, Mr. Naylor?'

'Certainly I did, sir. It has my name on it.'

'Do you remember anything about it?'

Mr. Naylor leaned on his counter with one hand, turning the watch over in the other.

'Come inside and sit down a minute,' he said. 'My leg won't let me stand for long.'

They went into the inner room, which seemed to be full of watches and parts of watches. It was a dingy, low-ceilinged place, with the indefinable smell of a workshop. An air of the past hung heavily over it.

'Do you still do all your own work?' Vickery said.

'Most of it. My customers don't like other people touching their watches.' Mr. Naylor sat down and took a closer look at the watch. 'Yes,' he said slowly at length, 'I do remember this watch. Dr. Oliphant bought it to give to the youngest Miss Faber. It was thought at one time that he would marry her, but nothing came of it. He was willing, I fancy. But she was a peculiar woman. Some years later she left Bath and I heard that she had gone to London. Has something happened to her?'

'It is probable that she is dead. I am trying to find out what I can about her.'

The sad blue eyes grew momentarily sadder. 'It is hard to think of Miss Delia—yes, that was her name, Delia—it is hard to think of her as dead. I remember her as she was forty years ago, sir, as bright and lively a woman as a man could wish for.'

'Is this Dr. Oliphant still alive?'

'Yes, he's very much alive. Retired now, but st l lives in Bath.'

'Do you know the address?'

'If he hasn't moved recently, and I hardly think he has, you'll find him in Russel Street. Quite a step from here and uphill all the way. Do you know Russel Street?'

'I can find my way there.'

Outside the constable was pacing up and down by the corner. 'Russel Street?' Vickery said.

'Up this way, sir. What number was it you wanted?'

'I don't know. Dr. Oliphant's house.'

The constable didn't know the number either. 'We can find out when we get there, sir.'

By the time Vickery got to Russel Street he was out of breath and conscious of his weight. It proved to be a sloping street, not very long or very wide, of tall, dignified houses. Vickery left the constable at the foot of the slope and walked up by himself.

A maid was standing at the door of one of the houses about half-way up, gazing down the street as though in expectation of a tradesman who had not arrived at the usual time.

'Dr. Oliphant's house?' Vickery asked her.

'Two doors further up on this side, sir.'

He began climbing again. Two doors up he rang the bell and asked for Dr. Oliphant. There was some delay before he was let in but not more than he had anticipated.

Dr. Oliphant received him affably in a room on the ground floor, a well-furnished room with high windows that looked out on the street. He was elderly but he carried his years lightly. His clean-cut face and confident, gentlemanly manner must have helped him a good deal in the practice from which he had now retired. There was nothing at all of the flaccidity of age about him.

'Miss Delia Faber?' he said. 'Yes, Inspector, I knew her well. But I haven't seen her for years. She left Bath, you know, and took herself off to London.'

'Were you her doctor?'

'I was both her doctor and her friend. I hope that your visit does not mean that she is in some sort of trouble.'

'I am not sure. Was Miss Faber's health good?'

'Perfect, at that time. She looked frail but she was actually as strong as a horse. Her only trouble, I remember, was a very slight lateral curvature of the spine. Nothing conspicuous, you understand, and not everybody knew about it. Naturally I would never have dreamed of referring to it today, if you had not been a police officer.'

That curvature, mentioned rather casually and without prompting, seemed like the light at the end of a tunnel. The watchmaker had made it clear that the Miss Fairford who had stayed at Cassilis Street must have been the Miss Faber of Bath. And now the doctor had confirmed that Miss Faber of Bath had had a curvature of the spine. Putting two and two together, it was pretty certain that the bones in the cellar had been Miss Delia Faber's. Or at least it was as near to certainty as anyone was likely to get.

'Had Miss Faber any friends in Bath?' Vickery enquired.

'At one time, yes. Hosts of friends. But none now, I should say. Time passes and people die. Whenever I have asked any of her old friends whether they have heard from her, the answer is always the same. They know nothing and have heard nothing.'

'Had she, before she left Bath, begun to behave rather oddly?'

The doctor took a little time to reply. 'As a matter of fact she had. It was a source of regret to her friends. We hoped that it would pass . . . And now, Inspector, might I know the purpose of these questions?'

'Certainly. Have you read of the Cassilis Street case in the papers?'

'Cassilis Street? The case in which a woman's skeleton was found in the cellar of a house somewhere in North London?'

'That is the one. I have reason to believe that the remains were those of Miss Delia Faber.'

Dr. Oliphant's clean-cut features seemed to sag. All at once he looked an old man.

'You mean that that was Delia?' he muttered. 'Poor little woman, poor little Delia . . . She was so gay, such a charming creature.'

His eyes filled with tears. For a while he sat slouched in his chair, staring at nothing. Then he blew his nose vigorously and pulled himself together.

'I am grieved to hear it,' he said. 'Most grieved. I can only hope that you are wrong.'

'From what you tell me, Doctor,' Vickery said, 'it seems probable that Miss Faber did not write to anybody in Bath in recent years. Would that, in your view, be correct?'

'Quite correct.'

'But she owned some property here, did she not?'

'She owned premises in New Bond Street. Alcock the draper has been the tenant for a good many years. I don't think she had any other property. Her father had been well-to-do at one time but there wasn't a great deal left when he died.'

'Hadn't she a solicitor to take care of her affairs?'

'Not for the last year or two that she lived here. As you already know she had begun to behave oddly even before she went off to London. One manifestation of this was that she suspected her solicitor of cheating her and took everything out of his hands. So far as I know she handled matters herself after that.'

Dr. Oliphant was looking more composed now. 'Do you know Bath well, Inspector?' he enquired politely.

'No. I have never been here before.'

'A delightful city. I would never live anywhere else. I cannot imagine what induced poor Delia Faber to leave it. I begged her to stay but it was useless. She had a bee in her bonnet about London. If she had stayed here among her friends she might have got over her queerness. She might have been as right as a trivet again by now.'

'She might well have been,' Vickery agreed. It was doubtful, he thought. In any case it was too late now. 'I must go and see Mr. Alcock the draper,' he said. 'New Bond Street, did you say?'

'Yes. It is a turning off Milsom Street. You can't miss the shop.'

A couple of minutes later Vickery was going down Russel Street to the foot of the slope, where he had left the constable.

'Where to now, sir?' said the constable.

'New Bond Street. A draper called Alcock.'

Down the hill they went again, past fine stone-built houses and expensive-looking shops. It was easier than going up and a good deal quicker.

Mr. Alcock's establishment looked as fashionable as any customer could desire, and it happened that Mr. Alcock himself was in front of his shop, bowing a lady across the pavement and into the gleaming chariot waiting in the roadway.

'I don't think I shall need you again,' Vickery told the constable. 'If I do I'll come along to the station.'

Mr Alcock was a spruce figure, as smart as his shop.

'Miss Faber?' he said. 'Yes, she still owns these premises. At least I suppose she does. We had better go upstairs, Inspector.' He summoned his shopwalker. 'I shall not be available for a while, Mr. Day. I do not wish to be disturbed.'

Vickery followed the draper upstairs. Everything was as stylish as the shop front and the proprietor. Mr. Alcock, like Dr. Oliphant, had evidently made a success of his life.

In a private sitting-room that might well have been in Mayfair, Mr. Alcock seated himself with care and said: 'I am most relieved to hear something of Miss Faber at last, Inspector. The matter of the rent was beginning to worry me. I couldn't think what to do. My lawyer advised me to do nothing and I followed his advice. But I wasn't easy about it. The money is ready and waiting but I had nowhere to send it. You know where Miss Faber is, do you?'

'She is dead.'

'Oh, dear, I am sorry to hear that. When did she die?'

'Probably in March last year.'

'Probably? Why only probably?'

'Because Miss Faber was almost certainly the victim in the Cassilis Street case.'

Mr. Alcock leaned back in his chair. 'Bless my soul,' he said. 'How very dreadful!'

'You have read about the case?'

'Yes. I was interested. I am a Londoner, you see, and my early days were spent not far from Cassilis Street.'

'Were you acquainted with Miss Faber?'

'I saw her frequently before she went to London. She was a rather strange lady.'

'In what way?'

'She fancied that people were trying to steal from her. She used to write to me before each quarter day, after she went to London, reminding me that the rent was due and giving me instructions as to how I was to send it. I had to send it to her care of a post office, where she would presumably call and collect it. She wouldn't have it sent to the house where she was living and in fact I had no notion where she lived, except that it seemed to be in London. I suppose she was afraid that somebody would open the letter and steal the money if she had it sent to her house or her lodgings or wherever it was that she lived. Even the post office was rarely the same. And the letter had to be addressed to certain initials, never to her by name.' Mr. Alcock got up and opened a bureau that stood in a corner of the room. 'I have always been strict in paying my debts, Inspector. You will see from this letter that I paid the rent for the March quarter last year on the 24th of March.'

He handed Vickery the letter. It was a formal note, a mere covering letter for the remittance. Pinned to it was an envelope post-marked March 24th at Bath and addressed to C.F., care of the Post Office, Holborn, London. It had been opened and endorsed at the post office, *Communication Not Claimed*, and returned to Mr. Alcock on the 24th April.

'Have you got Miss Faber's last letter?' Vickery asked.

The draper went to his bureau again.

'Here it is, Inspector.'

Vickery took the sheet of cheap, scented notepaper. The scent was stale now. The handwriting was florid. He had never seen Miss Faber's handwriting before, and he had nothing to compare this letter with. The letter bore no address or date. It was a reminder that the next quarter's rent was due on March 25th, together with the instruction about sending it to the Holborn Post Office.

'Something has been pinned to this,' he said.

'Yes. The envelope.'

'Do you always keep envelopes in that way?'

'Oh, dear me, no. Miss Faber was an exception. She was so peculiar, you see. It seemed a wise precaution in her case.'

'You still have the envelope, have you?'

Mr. Alcock produced it. 'Posted in London on March the 14th,' he said.

Vickery examined the envelope. There was nothing unusual about it. It had, as Alcock said, been stamped in London on the 14th of March. Miss Faber, it appeared, had been killed between the 14th and the 25th of March.

'These documents will be required in connection with the case,' he said.

'Very well.' Mr. Alcock hesitated. 'Shall I have to give evidence?'

'That is not for me to say.'

'I only wondered. I don't mind, of course. Except that it is so difficult for me to leave the business.'

'You will be informed.' Vickery heaved his bulk out of the chair. 'You are quite certain, are you, Mr. Alcock, that you never heard from Miss Faber again?'

'Absolutely certain, Inspector.'

Vickery walked back to his hotel, looking curiously about him. Bath, he decided, was in some respects not unlike the West End of London. There were the same terraces of tall symmetrical houses, with five floors including the attic and the basement, the same areas and area railings, the same parapets in front of the attic windows. And behind the stately houses there seemed to be the same little walled gardens. But the air, he thought, was not as bracing. He himself never felt so well as when he was in London.

All the way back in the train it rained hard, and it was still raining when he reached Paddington.

At his house in the best part of Kentish Town, his wife bustled around and got him a meal. Ada Vickery never forgot that her husband was the bread-winner.

'What is Bath like?' she asked him, when the meal was finished.

'Very hilly. Apart from that it is something like the West End of London on a small scale. There is even a street called New Bond Street.'

'Kentish Town is quite hilly enough for me,' she said. 'Did you get what you wanted at Bath?'

'I think so.' He drew a toothpick from his waistcoat pocket and used it thoughtfully. 'Yes. I know now who it was in that cellar. But I still don't know how she got there.'

4

Early next morning Vickery was at the Westminster House of Correction again.

'I want to go carefully through Martha Daniels' belongings,' he told Mr. Eccles. 'When I was here the other day I was mainly concerned with the watch. I should like to see the rest of her things now.'

'Can I have the watch back?' said Eccles.

'Here it is.'

Eccles took it and returned Vickery's receipt. 'I'll have the stuff brought in here,' he said. 'Was the watch useful?'

'Very.'

'Stupid of her to keep it. I suppose she couldn't bear to part with it.'

'Is she still docile?'

'Docile, yes. And more cheerful and healthy-looking than

she was. You seem to have done her good.'

Kitty Daniels' clothes and reticule and sundry possessions were brought in. Vickery went through them with a practised hand. The clothes were unimportant. The reticule and the sundry items were likely to prove more interesting.

'She doesn't seem to have had much,' he observed.

'No. That fellow she was living with took anything worth taking, I suppose.'

'Except the watch.'

'Yes, he overlooked that. There was a ring too, I fancy.'

Vickery examined the ring. 'Not worth much,' he said. 'She may have bought it herself. But I'll ask her about it. She didn't mention a ring to me.'

The reticule was disappointing. There were no letters, no names or addresses that might throw light on his problem. There was, however, a little book about the meaning of dreams. On the fly-leaf were the initials *C.F.* and *Bath 1850*. It was a worn little volume, that looked as if it had been consulted many times. And the handwriting on the fly-leaf was the florid handwriting of Miss Faber's letter to Mr. Alcock. Vickery put the book and the ring on one side. 'Can I see Martha Daniels now?' he said.

'When you like. Shall I take this stuff away?'

'Yes. Everything except the ring. And this little book.'

When Kitty Daniels came in he could see at once that Eccles had been right. Kitty had lost the dull and apathetic heaviness of a few days ago. The traces of dissipation were practically gone too. Her eye was lively, and she looked at him as a woman might look at a man who has taken her fancy.

'I have been going through your belongings,' he told her brusquely.

'I hope you enjoyed yourself, I'm sure.'

He ignored the pertness. 'This little book was Miss Fairford's, wasn't it?'

'Yes.'

'How did you come by it?'

'She gave it to me, the same way as she gave me the watch.'

'But you told me the other day that you had sold everything she gave you except the watch.'

'I forgot the book. But I wouldn't have got much for that, would I? There was a ring, too, that I forgot to mention. I suppose you found it. Miss Fairford gave me that too. I did try to sell that but nobody would give me more than a few shillings so I kept it.'

'Is this the ring?' Vickery said, putting it on the table.

'That's the one. You see, Miss Fairford was fond of me. We had our little tiffs but she was fond of me. That's why she gave me the things. But anyhow I don't see how it could possibly be Miss Fairford in the cellar because I saw her into a cab at the door myself, the day she left.'

'If it wasn't Miss Fairford in the cellar, who was it?'

'That's for you to find out, isn't it?' She paused as if something had just struck her. 'But I'll tell you this. There was a man in a room on the first floor for several weeks. It was a few months before Miss Fairford came. I forget his name but he was a man who had been abroad a lot. Mr. Berridge might remember him, though I doubt it. If I were to see the rent book it might bring the name back to me. Well, this man, as I say, had been abroad. He was a queer sort of man. I was half afraid of him, I can tell you. He kept a seven-chambered revolver in his room and he told me one day that he had a secret. Another day he offered me fifty pounds to go to America with him. But I wasn't taking that on. Not much I wasn't.'

Vickery stirred restlessly in his chair. 'What has all this got to do with the case?'

'Can't you be patient a bit? Another thing he told me was that he had a small house at Dulwich. He wanted me to go down there with him for a night. Of course I never did. But what I was going to mention was that one day I found a stain on his carpet. He said it was where he had upset a bottle of wine, but when I tried to wash it out it didn't seem like wine to me. It seemed more like blood. After he'd gone Mr. Berridge saw it and was annoyed with me for letting the man go without paying for the damage.'

'Is the carpet still there?'

'I don't know. You had better go back and see for yourself. It's my opinion that this man had had a woman up in his room and that she must have been done to death there. Then he must have got the body down to the cellar somehow. He was pretty strong, I should think. He could have done it easy enough.'

It was a tall story. All the same Vickery followed it up at Cassilis Street.

The Berridges had no recollection of the lodger with the revolver or the stain on the carpet. The rent-book suggested nothing as to the possible identity of the man. Even Nelly Cloke shook her head over the story. It was all Kitty's lies, she said.

'But talking about stains, mister,' she added, 'I did find a stain about the time Miss Fairford left. It was on a rug that was generally kept in Mr. Stephen's music-room.'

'Where is the rug now?'

'Goodness knows where it is now. I never saw it in the music-room after Miss Fairford went. But I did find it rolled up in Kitty's room. I could see it was stained because the stain had gone right through. She never caught me looking at it and at the time I didn't think much about it. As far as I remember I thought Kitty had upset something on the rug and took it up to her room so that nobody would find out.' Nelly's eyes glowed with sinister relish. 'I reckon it must have been blood, mister.'

'Didn't Mr. Berridge notice that the rug was gone?'

'Not that I ever heard tell. Nor Mrs. Berridge neither. But, bless you, they didn't know half what went on here. It was all left to Kitty.'

'Did you ever see the rug again, after you found it in Kitty's room?'

'No. Kitty must have got rid of it somehow pretty smart.'

Vickery went back to the Berridges with the story of the rug, but it was a bootless errand. Berridge recollected nothing. Mrs. Berridge thought she remembered that she had noticed at the time that the rug was gone and another put in its place. But Kitty did sometimes move the furniture around in that way, Mrs. Berridge said. There would have been nothing really unusual about it.

The second cellar seemed the obvious place for depositing the rug and Vickery had it searched again. But there was no rug there, nor anything that might once have been a rug.

At the House of Correction Kitty Daniels gave him no help.

'You've been talking to Nelly again, I can tell,' she said. 'There was a rug in the music-room, I agree, but it was taken away because it had got dingy, not because it was stained. Mr. Stephen asked if he could have a better one in the room, so I found him one.'

He got out his notebook.

'What did you do with the old rug?'

'I don't know what I did with it. Not now, I mean. Put it in the kitchen, perhaps. Or I might have given it to a man at the door. There was always men at the door for one thing or another.' Kitty's eyes narrowed. 'You're trying to pin this on me, aren't you?'

'I'm trying to find out the truth.'

'You're trying to pin it on me,' she repeated. 'Well, let me tell you right away, you're wasting your time. No jury would convict me just because I happened to have a watch and a ring and an old dream book in my possession. I never denied I had the things, did I? I told you straight out. And why? Because I was innocent, that's why. Why don't you go after the Berridges if you want a conviction? Not Mrs. Berridge. She wouldn't be mixed up in anything of the sort. But her husband might. Or Mr. Stephen. What was there to stop Mr. Berridge and Mr. Stephen doing away with some woman for the sake of her money? Why did Mr. Stephen go off in a hurry like he did? There must have been some good reason for it if you ask me.'

Her vehemence sent his eyebrows up. It was the first time he had heard her say a word against young Berridge.

'Always talking about the fine house he would have one day, Mr. Stephen was,' she went on. 'You can't have fine houses without money, can you? How do we know that he didn't get hold of some rich woman's money and then do the poor creature in?'

She began to hum a waltz tune to herself. Then, while he was writing in his notebook, she said: 'Do you know where Stephen Berridge is?'

'If I did know where he is, I couldn't tell you.'

'I don't think you do know. In fact I'm sure you don't. And you won't either. He's too clever for the police. He deceived everyone, including myself. I don't suppose he'll ever come back now. Woe betide him if he does. After he went off like that I made it my business to see a fellow called George Harris who worked at the same place. I knew this fellow, see, through Stephen. He wouldn't say anything to begin with, but afterwards he got tired and let on that, so far as he could make out, Stephen had another woman. He had no idea who it was, he said, and I'm inclined to believe him. Stephen wasn't one to give any secrets away, I can tell you that.'

For a moment she seemed to be on the brink of a major disclosure, then her eyes filled with mocking laughter. She had got him interested. He had almost begun to think that, after all, young Berridge really had had something to do with the skeleton in the cellar. But the moment passed. She was only making game of him. There was nothing definite to connect Stephen Berridge with the crime. But there were several things to connect Kitty Daniels with it. The watch, for example. And the evidence that Nelly Cloke would give.

'Have you questioned George Harris?' Kitty said.

'Mr. Berridge told me about Harris,' he admitted. 'Enquiries showed that he had left the music firm a year ago.'

Walking dispiritedly away from the House of Correction afterwards, Vickery came to the conclusion that it was time for him to make his report. He had got as much as he was likely to get. Others would have to decide on the next step.

His written report on the case would give him considerable trouble, mainly because his own mind was not made up. It was not even absolutely certain that the remains were in fact those of the woman who had once been the charming Miss Delia Faber. There was so little left with which to establish identification. The poor woman had cut herself off from her friends and relatives for so long. No living relations could be traced, and there was no evidence that she had had a bank account anywhere. What would happen to the ownership of the shop at Bath now, Vickery didn't know, but that wasn't his problem. His problem was to find the woman's murderer and he felt that he had failed.

That evening he talked the matter over with Ada his wife. This was something that he often did. He had found from experience that she was entirely discreet. Nothing that he told her about his cases ever passed beyond the four walls of their home. And occasionally she had hit a nail on the head, a nail that he himself had unaccountably missed.

'What happened to this Miss Fairford's clothes?' Ada asked. 'Apart from the odds and ends that Kitty Daniels admitted to, I mean. Do you suppose Kitty Daniels kept them and took them away with her when she left Cassilis Street?'

'We've made enquiries all over London at second-hand clothes shops. But it was hopeless, so long after the event. Women like Kitty Daniels are going to those shops with clothes all the time—cast-offs of the lady of the house, and so on. And generally speaking the people who keep the shops don't like the police much. It is bad for trade if they are thought to be hand in glove with the police. I reckon Kitty must have kept the clothes until after she left Cassilis Street at any rate. Perhaps Charley Owen got rid of them for her somehow when she went to live with him.'

'Has this Charley Owen been questioned?'

'Yes. We knew where to find him. He's been known to the police for years. But he wouldn't say a word that was of any use to us.'

Ada yawned. 'I don't think Kitty Daniels did it,' she said. 'Not by herself anyhow.'

'Who did then?'

'Young Berridge, if you ask me. Goodness knows how or why. But he didn't go off in all that hurry without a good reason. Telling those lies about it to everybody too. He's the man you ought to get hold of.'

'We've tried. He's simply vanished.'

'Kitty Daniels must have known about it,' said Ada. 'And she's shielding Stephen Berridge now. Even though he went off like that and left her to face the music. Some women are fools, I must say. I wouldn't swing for any man.'

Vickery's report concluded with the submission that there was insufficient evidence against Kitty Daniels, and that no other suspect was known. Except Stephen Berridge, who could not be traced. And he was only suspected because he had been on the premises at the time, had been on friendly terms with the victim and had mysteriously disappeared at about the assumed time of the murder. There was, in addition, the matter of the stained rug from his music-room. If Stephen Berridge had turned up, these points might have led to something. But he hadn't turned up. And nobody, so far, had been able to turn him up. Vickery recommended that no charge should be made against Kitty Daniels, and that further efforts should be made to discover the whereabouts of Stephen Berridge.

His recommendations were not accepted. The woman Martha Daniels, also known as Kitty Daniels, should, he was instructed, be charged with the murder of Cordelia Faber, also known as Delia Fairford.

He swore quietly to himself, went to the House of Correction again, and carried out his instructions.

Kitty Daniels shrugged, and replied that she understood. There was no scene, no fuss. He said what he had to say, and the wardress took her away.

7

I

THE TRIAL of Martha Daniels took place fairly early in the new year and occupied two days.

Frank Unwin was in court during the whole of the trial. He was a freelance writer, a hack who made his living mainly from criminal cases. A good deal of his writing was done for the *Illustrated Police News,* which presented crime and criminals in a style that the meanest intelligence could appreciate. As there was never any lack of crimes or of mean intelligences, Unwin was rarely without work.

He lived at Camberwell, in a respectable street just off the Walworth end of the Camberwell Road, and he was the sole support of his mother. A bachelor of fifty now, he had supported his mother for twenty-five years, ever since the death of his father. In his younger days he had thought of marrying. But he had given up the idea long ago. He couldn't really afford to maintain two women. Nor did he feel himself capable of dealing successfully with the troubles that were likely to ensue if he brought a wife into his mother's home.

So he had gone on living with Ma. It had been a comfortable existence, that might have continued indefinitely, but for one difficulty that had grown to be a worry to him during the past year. Ma was becoming old and infirm and forgetful. She was, in fact, getting on for eighty.

He was a little man, mild and easy-going. When he brushed

his thinning hair in front of the glass in the morning he saw, as often as not, a cheerful face and a humorous eye. He sometimes wondered how he had managed to keep a face like that, after a life spent largely in writing about felons. One might have expected a certain look of felony to have rubbed off on him.

As he journeyed from Camberwell on the first day of the trial, he wondered what sort of dirty hussy this Martha Daniels would prove to be. Women in the dock were mostly hussies, in his experience. But it was, after all, the hussies who provided him with his living, not the good women.

If Martha Daniels got off, he had a proposition to make to her. From what he had heard and read, it seemed possible that she might be free in a day or two, but one could never be sure.

One of the most successful Q.C.s in London had been briefed for the defence. It was rumoured that the defence costs were being paid by a wealthy gentleman living abroad. Martha Daniels had been a housemaid in good service at one time, it was said, and the story was going round that this gentleman had employed her some years ago, when he had had a house in town. The man, whoever he was, had seen the reports of the Cassilis Street case in the English newspapers, and had given his solicitors instructions that the accused woman was to have the best defence that money could buy. His identity, however, was to be kept secret.

The rumour gave an added flavour to the case. There were those who alleged that the prisoner had been the gentleman's mistress, and Frank Unwin thought this not unlikely.

When he saw Martha Daniels in the dock he had to admit that she didn't look like a hussy. A self-respecting upper housemaid, he thought she looked. Her manner was composed and demure, but that didn't mean that she wasn't a hussy. Some of the worst hussies were demure enough till you found them out. A tallish woman she was, probably in the early thirties.

The trial, after a slow start, got into its stride.

Frank Unwin had a good memory, that had served him well in his work. But when he thought about the cases that he had sat through, he never recalled them in consecutive detail. His memories were of moments and personalities, clear enough in his mind but hardly ever in their right order. It was the same with the trial of Martha Daniels.

John Berridge, the lodging-house keeper, he remembered as a fine-looking man, the sort that women were supposed to admire. Defence counsel evidently felt that the fellow was being too eager to incriminate Martha Daniels and sought to discredit him.

'When did you first meet the prisoner?' counsel enquired.

'At my shop in Tottenham Court Road.'

'You have a shop, have you? What sort of shop?'

'I deal in second-hand furniture.'

'Did Martha Daniels come to buy furniture?'

'No. She came on behalf of her employer, a lady who was then living in Brunswick Square. This lady wished to sell some furniture.'

Defence counsel, who had the face of an old satyr, asked whether it was on that occasion that Martha Daniels agreed to come to the house in Cassilis Street.

'Not on that occasion, no,' Berridge replied.

'Where did you next see her?'

'At her employer's house in Brunswick Square.'

'Were those the only two occasions on which you saw Martha Daniels, before she was installed at Cassilis Street?'

'No. I saw her several times.'

'Did you take her to Brighton one day?'

The tall, good-looking man flinched and hesitated.

'Did you take her to Brighton?' counsel persisted.

'Yes.'

'Did you spend a night there with her?'

'Yes.'

'And did you have intimate relations with her on that occasion?'

'Yes.'

Berridge's shoulders were drooping. His replies could hardly be heard.

'Did you,' counsel pursued, 'engage this young woman as a housemaid in order that your intimacy with her might be continued more conveniently under your own roof?'

'No.' The witness showed a flash of resentment. 'I did not.'

'But was the intimacy continued after she came to your house?'

'To some extent, yes.'

'To what extent, Mr. Berridge?'

'Only now and then. And only at first.'

Counsel was satisfied. He had made his point. John Berridge was revealed as a lecher who had seduced a young woman at Brighton and persuaded her to come and live in his house. The jury would justifiably assume that the young woman had been much under Berridge's influence. Martha Daniels, there in the dock, looked the part of the once innocent maidservant to the life. And John Berridge, with his dark, mature good looks, was well cast for the seducer's rôle. The jury would not fail to note all this. Whatever the prisoner might have done, the impression was conveyed that she was being made a scapegoat for somebody else, possibly Berridge himself.

The Attorney General stressed Berridge's orders to his shopboy to clear the cellar. Would any guilty man have done such a thing, knowing that a woman's remains were in the cellar? It seemed unanswerable. But it didn't mean that it was Martha Daniels who had put the woman's body there.

Mrs. Berridge was nervous and flustered in the witness box. Asked about the date of Miss Fairford's assumed departure from Cassilis Street, she replied that it must have been about the same time that Stephen went away, she thought.

'Who was Stephen?' blandly enquired the defence counsel.

'My stepson Stephen. Mr. Berridge's son by his first wife, you understand.'

'Why did Stephen go away, Mrs. Berridge?'

'We don't know at all. He just went off. It was most unexpected.'

'And where did he go?'

'We didn't know that either. He just ran away, it seemed.'

'Had he resided in your house before he went away?'

'Oh yes, he had always lived at home with us. We had no idea that he gambled, but of course he must have gone off suddenly like that because of a debt of honour. I don't see what else it could have been.'

At the recollection of the unhappy episode the poor woman could hardly keep back the tears. The judge was looking as if he doubted the relevance of all this.

'Why do you suppose,' counsel asked, 'that a gambling debt was the reason for your stepson's going away so suddenly?'

'Well, it couldn't have been anything else, could it?'

'I am asking you, Mrs. Berridge. Why do you assume that there was a gambling debt?'

'It just seemed that it must be so,' she faltered.

'Had you any evidence of such a debt?'

'No, no evidence. It was just that there was no other possible reason for his going off like that.' She put one hand to her bosom and swayed slightly in the box. 'Excuse me, my heart is pounding so dreadfully. I suffer from palpitations, you see.'

The judge allowed her to be seated and spoke to her kindly. Defence counsel resumed:

'Was your stepson on friendly terms with Miss Fairford?' he asked.

'Oh, quite friendly. That is to say, she liked to hear him play the piano and he used to let her come and sit in his music-room while he played. Stephen played very well.'

'Did she set her cap at him, by any chance?'

Mrs. Berridge looked shocked. 'Dear me, no. Miss Fairford was more than old enough to be his mother. Much more.'

'Have you ever seen anything of an affectionate nature between them?'

'Not affectionate. He was always pleasant with her.'

'Did your stepson ever ask you for money?'

'No. He seemed to have enough. He had a good position in the West End.'

'Were you aware that Miss Fairford had offered him money?'

'Certainly not. And I don't believe she ever did!'

'Thank you, Mrs. Berridge.'

Frank Unwin wondered whether the attempt to direct the jury's attention to the missing stepson had succeeded. There was certainly something very peculiar about the behaviour of this piano-playing fellow.

The Attorney General left the stepson alone. The distinguished law officer of the Crown was a player who generally, by repute, liked to have a card up his sleeve, a polished performer with a deceptively negligent style. Whether there was a winning card today or not, his easy, detached manner would be the same.

'Now, Mrs. Berridge,' he smiled, 'the jury would probably like to know something about the management of the lodging-house during the time when the accused was in your service.' He sounded urbanely unconcerned. 'Did you manage it yourself?'

'No, I can't say that I did.' The witness was basking gratefully in the Attorney General's mildness. 'I am afraid that I left everything to Kitty.'

'Kitty?'

'Kitty Daniels. Her name is Martha, I know, but she was always called Kitty.'

'Can you tell the jury what Kitty did?'

'Oh, really, she did practically everything. With the help

of the girl, of course. Kitty was always so obliging.'

There was a titter in the court and the judge called for silence. 'Pray continue, Mrs. Berridge,' he said.

The witness embarked upon a recital of Kitty Daniels' excellent qualities. Kitty had been so hard-working, so honest, so capable, so cheerful and pleasant to have about the house. One could never have supposed, listening to Edith Berridge, that her husband had been forced to admit, in front of everybody, that Kitty Daniels had been his mistress.

'Did you go round the house regularly, making sure that everything was in order?' asked the Attorney General.

'There was no need. Things went so smoothly.'

'Did you know when lodgers left and new lodgers came?'

'Well, yes, we were told that. Kitty always told my husband or myself.'

'Did you see Miss Fairford leaving the house?'

'No. I must have been out, I think. I don't remember seeing her go.'

The Attorney General looked doubtful. But at least he had established the point that Martha Daniels had been in a position to do pretty much as she liked at Cassilis Street, so long as things went well, which apparently they always did . . .

Three witnesses from Bath took the stand. Their evidence was intended to satisfy the jury that the remains in the cellar were indeed those of the elderly spinster with girlish airs who had come from Bath to London, who had been known at Cassilis Street as Miss Fairford and whose watch had been found in the possession of the accused. A lame watchmaker; a retired doctor; a spruce draper: they gave their evidence and stood down. There appeared to be little doubt that the remains had in fact been those of the eccentric Miss Faber or Fairford, formerly of Bath.

Frank Unwin sometimes wished that the law allowed an accused person in a criminal case to go into the witness-box. He would have liked, for instance, to see Martha

Daniels in the box. Unless he was much mistaken, she would have been more than a match for the prosecution. It seemed unfair that a woman should have to stand in the dock and say nothing, while other people might be swearing her life away. Perhaps one day the law would be changed.

A boy named Baxter, who had apparently been the one to discover the remains, was called to the stand and gave his evidence with Cockney confidence. The jurymen seemed to like him. Frank Unwin liked him too. He had been a Cockney boy himself, years ago.

Then Lizzie Siddle, a scraggy woman who had taken Kitty Daniels' place at the lodging-house, gave her account of the way in which the house was managed when she first went there. It was a bald statement. Neither the Attorney General nor the defence counsel got anything out of Lizzie beyond the few plain words that she considered sufficient. . . .

Frank Unwin went home at the close of the first day of the trial and found that during the day his old mother had had a fall in the scullery. She seemed not to have broken any bones but she was bruised and shaken. She insisted on hobbling about to get a meal for him and refused to permit him to call in a neighbour or summon the doctor. Ma had always been difficult and independent and she got worse as she got older. But he was fond of her and, he hoped, kind to her. If she sometimes exasperated him, he never let her see that he was put out. Her position at the centre of his life was impregnable.

She was no better next morning but she got up early and saw to it that he had his breakfast. He tried to help her with the breakfast things but she asked him what the hell he thought he was doing. Ma had never been a chapel-going woman.

Ill at ease he went back to the court for the second day of the trial. Before he left he made Ma promise that she would rest as much as possible, but he knew very well that unless she felt half dead she would do nothing of the sort.

He might be very late coming home, he told her. . . .

The police inspector, a bulky, slow-moving man called Vickery with traces of a provincial accent, was the first witness that day. He described how the accused had been found in the Westminster House of Correction.

'Why was she there?' enquired the Attorney General.

'She was serving a sentence for theft.'

'Did you make an examination of her possessions?'

'I did, sir.'

'And did you find among her possessions anything that had apparently once belonged to Miss Fairford?'

'Yes. A watch. The watch referred to by Dr. Oliphant and Mr. Naylor in their evidence.'

'Anything else, Inspector?'

'A ring. And a book about the meaning of dreams.'

There was a ripple of amusement in the court.

'Were you satisfied that the watch and the ring and the book about dreams had formerly been in the possession of Miss Fairford?'

'Yes, sir.'

'What action did you take to satisfy yourself, Inspector?'

The police officer told the jury what he had learned from Nelly Cloke, a general servant employed at the lodging-house; from the witnesses whom he had talked to at Bath; and from his conversations with the accused at the House of Correction. He gave his evidence with the professional detachment of one who had given evidence many times before in other cases.

Defence counsel enquired particularly regarding the conversations at the House of Correction.

'When you first talked to the accused, Inspector, were you aware that she had had in her possession the watch which, we are told, previously belonged to Miss Fairford?'

'I did not know for certain. I only knew what Nelly Cloke had told me about such a watch.'

'Did you challenge the accused on the point?'

'No. She admitted that she had the watch.'

'Before you even mentioned it?'

'Yes. To the best of my recollection, I asked, following up something that Nelly Cloke had said, whether Miss Fairford had been a mean woman. The accused replied that the exact reverse was the case. Miss Fairford, she said, had given her several things, including a watch.'

The point was made. Martha Daniels had not tried to conceal the fact that she had the watch. She had admitted having it before the Inspector had asked about it. A good point, as far as it went.

The Attorney General tried to blunt the point. 'Did the accused know, at the time of this conversation, that you might have examined her belongings and found the watch among them?'

'She could hardly have known that. She might have suspected it.'

The burden of proof, in Frank Unwin's opinion, was going to be too heavy a load for the Crown to carry successfully in this case. He began to worry about Ma and wondered what time it would be when he got back to Camberwell. It was stuffy in the court. Martha Daniels, he noticed, was looking tired. The strain was telling on her.

Nelly Cloke, the general at the lodging-house, had got herself up for the occasion, and in addition to her Sunday best she wore an air of pleasurable excitement. Once she glanced towards the dock with a smirk of triumph which the prisoner met with a cold, contemptuous stare. It was evident that the humble general felt the eyes of the world upon her.

Yet she proved to be a bad witness, garrulous and irrelevant. It was hard to pin her down to a fact. And her scraps of hearsay, spiteful asides and innuendoes were so frequent that the judge had to warn her to mind her words and do no more than reply to the questions put to her by counsel.

There was a story about a stained rug. And another about a smell coming from the cellar.

'But when I said something about the smell Kitty told me to get on with my work and made other remarks that I wouldn't care to repeat. She didn't want me in that cellar, that was my opinion and still is.'

'Regarding the rug,' said the Attorney General, 'will you tell the jury where you found the rug.'

'In Kitty's room, where it shouldn't have been. It was the rug belonging to Mr. Stephen's music-room, and there was blood on it. Kitty must have taken it upstairs to her room.'

'How did you know that it was blood on the rug?'

'I know blood when I see it, don't I? If it wasn't blood, why should it be hidden away up there?'

The Attorney General was patient.

'When did you find the stained rug in the prisoner's room?' he enquired.

'About the time Miss Fairford left. The time she was supposed to leave, I mean. And another thing, mister. Kitty sent me out shopping on the morning when Miss Fairford was supposed to have left. When I come back, Miss Fairford is gone, Kitty tell me. Now what do you make of that?'

Nobody could make much of it or of Nelly. All the same, Frank Unwin had the feeling that there might be something in what Nelly Cloke had been trying, in her confused way, to say. Somewhere in the welter of disorderly words might be the truth about Miss Fairford.

The Attorney General's closing speech was dry and legal. He relied on the circumstances that the prisoner had had an opportunity to commit the crime, by reason of her position in the house, and that some of Miss Fairford's property had been found in the prisoner's possession. There was no evidence connecting any other person with the crime.

Frank Unwin knew that this sort of reasoning had sent more than one prisoner to the gallows. It was too neat and made-to-measure for his liking. He doubted whether it would do the prosecution's business for them.

Defence counsel had a confidential man-to-man style with the jury. Was it conceivable, he asked, that the accused, without help from any other person, could have killed Miss Fairford and dragged or carried the corpse down to the cellar? The Crown's theory, he submitted, assumed more than it was reasonable to assume. He, for his part, asked the jury to accept the prisoner's account of the matter as a much more natural explanation. What could be more reasonable than that Miss Fairford should leave the house in the usual way? And what more natural than that the accused should be the only one to see her go? After all, the accused had been practically in charge of the house. The prosecution attached great importance to the fact that the accused was later found to have in her possession a watch, a ring and a dream book formerly belonging to the deceased. But the accused said that Miss Fairford had given them to her. And why not? Elderly people frequently became fond of the servants who ministered to their needs and comforts and this fondness often found expression in gifts. It was clear that the accused had been a most capable servant. And the jury could see for themselves that she was a woman of considerable charm. But, says the prosecution, the remains of Miss Fairford were in fact discovered in the cellar. So that she could not have gone off in a cab . . . Why could she not have gone off in a cab? How is anyone to know where she died and how? Could not Miss Fairford have been done to death after she left the house in Cassilis Street? And could not the body have been secretly deposited in the cellar of the house in Cassilis Street in order to cast suspicion on one or more of the persons residing in that house? Counsel submitted that there was no case to go to the jury and asked for the prisoner's release forthwith. The charge of murder, he claimed, had not been brought home. . . .

A good speech, Frank Unwin considered. Whoever it was that was paying for the defence had got his money's worth.

The judge's summing-up was cautious. He took the jury through the evidence but did little more. They must make up their own minds about it, he told them.

The jurymen did so, in less than half an hour.

'Not guilty,' said the foreman.

Martha Daniels, pale in the dock, heaved a sigh of relief. The colour returned to her cheeks. It was over. A wardress handed her a bottle of smelling-salts.

Frank Unwin hurried round to the side door by which, he knew from experience, Martha Daniels might be expected to leave the court. It was nearly half past eight.

2

He thought, as he waited outside the court, of his mother. It was dark and getting late. Ma had never needed coddling. But she was old. She had to be looked after, whether she liked it or not.

Several other people were waiting by the side door but there was no crowd. The door opened, sending a shaft of light across the pavement. But it wasn't the woman he was waiting for. A man came out, then two men together. It was twenty past nine when Martha Daniels appeared.

She was alone.

'Excuse me, Miss Daniels,' he began, raising his hat.

'Who are you?' she said. She glanced round with an air, he thought, of disappointment, as though she felt that, in all London, there ought to have been one friend waiting outside for her. 'I don't know you, do I?' she added, peering at his face.

'No, you don't know me. My name is Unwin, Frank Unwin. I write for the *Illustrated Police News* and I should like you to give me your life story. And the truth about the Cassilis Street case too.'

'Go to hell. I want to forget the whole thing.'

'But the public hasn't forgotten it, Miss Daniels. If you don't tell me what you know, I shall have to make it up myself, and that wouldn't be so interesting.'

She stared at him. 'Do you mean that you would print a lot of lies?'

'Oh, well, we know what readers of the *Illustrated Police News* enjoy and we give it to them. Nothing wrong in that, is there? You will tell me something, I'm sure. Something to go on, so that I don't have to make it all up.'

'No,' she said. 'You can do what you like. But I've had enough of Cassilis Street. I won't have anything to do with it.'

'It means money,' he pointed out.

She hesitated. 'How much?'

'Fifteen pounds.'

He waited anxiously for her reaction to this.

'All right,' she said at last, 'if you'll give me a sovereign on account now.'

He gave her the sovereign. 'Have you got anywhere to go to?'

'No. But I can get in somewhere now that I've got this money of yours.'

'I suppose so. I expect you're feeling a bit lost, Miss Daniels. People who have been in prison have told me that they do feel rather lost when they are let out. Why not come to my house, Miss Daniels, just for tonight?'

He was afraid for a moment that she would flounce off in a huff, then she looked up and down the chilly street and said: 'Are you married?'

'No. I live with my mother.'

'Where?'

'Camberwell.'

'Nobody else in the house?'

'No. Only my mother and me.'

She seemed to come to a decision. 'Well, I know how to

look after myself, so I may as well try it, I suppose. How many bedrooms are there in this house?'

'Three. Ma's, mine and the spare room.'

'What will your mother think about you bringing a strange woman home?'

'Ma will understand. She knows that I have to do this sort of thing in the way of business.'

'You mean that you've taken women home before like this?'

'Several times, yes. And men too. Sometimes I take them to a public house. It depends on the circumstances.'

She laughed, throwing her head back. It did not seem possible that this was the same woman who, so very recently, had stood white-faced in the dock.

'You're a funny one,' she said. And then, briskly: 'Let's go, then, if we're going. I'm getting cold.'

He hailed a cab and they set off together, over the dark river and on to Elephant and Castle and the small house at Camberwell where Ma would be waiting.

'Your mother must be a good age,' Martha Daniels said. 'How old are you? About fifty-five?'

'Fifty. Ma's getting on for eighty.'

She put her head on one side and smiled sweetly. 'Proper little mother's boy,' she remarked.

He felt himself flush. 'No need to be nasty, Miss Daniels.'

'Sorry, Mr.—— What did you say your name was?'

'Unwin. Frank Unwin.'

'I didn't mean to upset you.' She closed her eyes, while the cab-horse jogged on its way. 'Life's a queer game,' she said. 'Not much more than an hour ago I was in that court thinking that before long they might hang me. I knew I was innocent, of course, but what difference would that have made? No difference at all, as you know as well as what I do . . . And now I'm as free as air and going to Camberwell in a cab with a man I'd never set eyes on till tonight. And not for the usual reason either . . . You are a one, I must say. Taking home a woman like me to see your mother.'

'What's wrong with you?'

'What's wrong with me? Weren't you in court during the trial?'

'Yes. All the time.'

'Then you know that I've been in prison for theft, for one thing. And you heard what Mr. Berridge said about him and me, for another. And on top of all that, there are those who still think I killed that poor old dolly at Cassilis Street. That's not the sort of woman a man generally takes home to see his mother.'

'I told you before,' he said, 'that my mother knows perfectly well that I sometimes have to take all sorts of people home, in connection with my work. You don't suppose I like it, do you?'

He was tired, and the unaccustomed sharpness of his tone showed it.

'Sorry, Mr. Unwin,' she said. 'Are we nearly there?'

The cab turned a corner into a side-street.

'Practically there now,' he said.

A couple of minutes later he was paying the cabby. Martha Daniels gazed up at the front of the house.

'Looks respectable,' she remarked.

'It is respectable.'

He got out his latch-key. He was still worrying about Ma. And he was hardly inside the door when he saw her, lying at the foot of the stairs, apparently conscious but unable to move.

'Is that you, Frank?' she demanded feebly.

'Yes, Ma.' He was down beside her in a moment. 'What happened?'

'I fell again . . . Slipped . . . Bloody old goose I am . . . Who's that with you?'

'Miss Daniels.'

The old woman continued to swear softly to herself. Then she said: 'Who's Miss Daniels?'

Frank Unwin felt that he was near the end of his tether. He didn't know what to do. Ma was a biggish woman and he was a small man. He couldn't possibly carry her upstairs. But he couldn't leave her where she was either.

'Miss Daniels is a friend of mine,' he said irritably.

Martha Daniels confirmed this. 'That's right,' she said. 'I'm a friend of Frank's. And it's a good job I'm here, if you ask me. Now, let's get you up to bed, Mrs. Unwin . . . Gently, now, that's better . . .'

She was strong and capable, and she seemed to know just what to do. Presently Ma was in bed.

'I had a giddy fit,' Ma said. 'Tell the truth I'm not sure what happened. It wasn't long before you come in, Frank. I'd pretty well given you up for tonight and I was going up to bed.' She turned her head away from her son to take a good look at Martha Daniels. 'You in trouble, dear?' she enquired.

Martha Daniels hedged. 'What sort of trouble do you mean?'

'I didn't mean in the family way. But the people Frank brings here have mostly been in trouble. They tell him their stories and he writes it all down. It's money for us and money for them. He's clever, my Frank is . . . Now leave me, please, both of you. There's some supper in the kitchen. I'm perfectly all right and I don't want anyone fussing over me. And if Frank sends for the doctor he'll get the length of my tongue and that's flat . . . Have you shown your friend the spare room, Frank?'

'Not yet, Ma. I will, later on.'

'That's right. The room's all ready. But make sure the pot's under the bed.' She winked at her son's guest. 'What do they call you, dear?'

'Kitty.'

'Kitty, that's nice. Yes, I like that. Well, good-night, Kitty. Frank will look after you. He's a good boy, Frank is.'

They went downstairs and sat in the kitchen, eating cold beef and drinking porter.

'Ma's taken to you,' he told Kitty, when they had finished.

'Gad to hear it, I'm sure . . . God, I'm tired. I could drop off sitting here.' She yawned widely. 'Where's this spare room of yours?'

'Next to Ma's . . . You must be completely knocked up, Miss Daniels.'

'I am knocked up and no mistake. And for God's sake call me Kitty.'

'You'll tell me the story tomorrow, won't you?' he pleaded.

'Yes, I'll tell you something. Now show me the bedroom.' She yawned again and got up from the table. 'Will your mother be all right, do you think?'

'I expect so. I'll look in at her during the night.'

'That's a good boy. Come on then.'

The spare room seemed cold to him. 'Are you going to be warm enough here?' he said.

'I've slept soundly in colder places than this. I shan't need rocking.' Kitty lifted the valance of the bed and peered underneath. 'There's two there,' she said, giggling foolishly as if she were not far from hysteria.

In the candle-light she was quite a pretty woman, prettier than he had realised before.

'Good-night,' he said.

'Good-night . . . And thank you. I don't know what I should have done without you tonight.'

He was half afraid that she was going to kiss him.

'If I hadn't had you with me,' he said, backing nervously out, 'I don't know what I should have done about Ma.'

He didn't want to seem too grateful, because he had to get that story out of her first thing tomorrow morning. And gratitude, in his opinion, wasn't a good basis for a business transaction.

3

He woke in the small hours and tip-toed to Ma's room. She was asleep, so he crept back. When he opened his eyes again it was getting light and he could hear someone moving about below. Pulling on his trousers he went to investigate.

Ma was still in bed. 'Oh, it's you, is it?' she said, as he put his head round the door. 'I thought it might be Kitty. She came in just now to see if I needed anything. She says I've got to stop here for a bit.'

'How did you sleep, Ma?'

'Pretty fairish. Kitty said she'd get the breakfast. I told her where the things were. And that you weren't to be disturbed.'

He listened for a moment to the reassuring sounds that still came from the kitchen. 'Nice to have someone just now to help you with the work,' he said.

His mother did not comment on this proposition. 'It's these giddy fits,' she grumbled. 'I can't trust meself. I suppose I'll have to get the doctor to give me a bottle to put me right.'

He dressed quickly, thinking as he did so that Ma must surely be frightened about herself. A woman like Ma didn't let another woman come into her kitchen and get the breakfast unless she was frightened. Two giddy fits, one after the other, had scared her, even to the point of agreeing to have a bottle from the doctor. And letting Kitty get the breakfast. Never before had Ma consented to have a servant in the house, not even a daily woman to do the scrubbing.

Kitty, down in the kitchen, had her sleeves rolled up.

'Getting on like a house afire,' she said.

'Can I help you? I know where everything is kept.'

'I'll ask if I want to know anything. You go and read the paper. I don't like men around when I'm working.'

They had breakfast together, after she had taken a tray

up to Ma. Later, while Kitty was washing up, he walked along to the doctor's house and presently the doctor drove up to the door.

The doctor's conclusion was that there was nothing much wrong with Ma, apart from her age, which couldn't be cured. The giddy fits were nature's warning that she must take things easy. She ought to stay in bed for a week and after that get up late every day and do as little as possible. He proposed to give her some pills. But it was primarily rest that she needed.

'She's always done all her own housework,' Frank Unwin objected.

'Well, she can't do it any more. You must get someone to help her. What about that pleasant woman who opened the door to me? Who is she? A neighbour?'

'A friend.'

'Can she stay for a while, until you hear of somebody else?'

'I don't know. I hardly think so.'

'Well, you ask her. She seemed to me to be just what you need.'

Ma grumbled when her son went up to the bedroom after the doctor had driven off.

'All doctors are the same. A meddling lot, one and all. I tell you what, Frank. I'll stay here today and no longer. Tomorrow I'm getting up as usual.'

Afterwards he told Kitty what the doctor had said, together with his mother's remarks. He was worried.

'Your mother'll never be able to do what she did before,' was Kitty's opinion.

'In that case,' he hesitated, 'would you stop on here for a while?'

She wasted no words over the matter. 'I don't mind obliging for a time,' she said. 'Till you get someone else, that is . . . And cheer up, can't you? Care killed the cat, you know.'

He was relieved. The future of his domestic life was at any rate temporarily assured.

'Can we talk about that story now?' he begged.

'Oh, you and your precious story!'

'It's my living. It's money.'

'All right. What is it you want then? You tell me while I do these potatoes.'

He assumed his professional mantle. 'I shall want to know your age, where you were born, who your parents were, what you were doing before you took the situation in Cassilis Street——'

'That sounds pretty dull,' she interrupted. 'But I could tell you some tales of life below stairs that ought to suit your readers to a T.'

'Capital. I must use your name, though. They must be your stories. It's the name that counts, you see, and your having been the central figure in a murder trial.'

'Fair's fair. You can use my name.' She laughed. 'Secrets of Kitty Daniels.'

'And what about the secrets of Cassilis Street?'

She stopped peeling the potato and leaned both elbows on the kitchen table. 'I've been thinking about that,' she said. 'I'll tell you about Miss Fairford as I knew her. And just mention the Berridges. But nothing to take away their characters. Understand?'

He put down his pencil. 'You promised. For fifteen pounds, you said.'

'Well, I changed my mind, that's all. Look here, I can make your story spicy enough without dragging the Berridges through the muck again. I wouldn't care so much if it was only Mr. Berridge. But it wouldn't be fair to Missus, who was always good to me. Or Miss Ruth.'

'Or Mr. Stephen?' he suggested.

'Or Mr. Stephen, if it comes to that.' Her eyes were stormy. 'I won't drag them through the muck,' she repeated obstinately.

He returned to the charge. 'I could very well write up a lot of stuff about them as though it had come from you,' he pointed out. 'And you couldn't stop me, could you?'

'I couldn't stop you but I could do one or two other things.' She pushed back her chair and got up. Then she untied her apron and stood menacingly over him with arms akimbo. 'To begin with, I could walk out of here and leave you and your mother in the lurch. And later on I could arrange matters so that you would be found in a cellar with your head bashed in and a rope round your neck. That's one or two things I could do, Mr. Frank Unwin.'

He quailed before her . . . So she had done that Cassilis Street murder. She had been guilty all the time. And now in a fit of temper she had let it out. He sat there tongue-tied. All he could think of was that he and Ma might have been murdered in their beds last night.

Then as he stared up at her, she began to giggle. The giggle swelled to a helpless laugh and she had to sit down until it was over, letting the laugh have its way with her. At last, her shoulders still shaking, the tears of intense amusement trickling down her face, she managed to say: 'My, you aren't half easy to have on.'

He was put out. 'You are a bitch, Kitty Daniels.'

That merely made her start giggling again. 'You really thought I done that murder, didn't you?'

'Just for the moment, yes.'

'You don't think so now?'

'No, I don't think so now.'

This was only half true. But on the whole he thought it pretty certain that the fit of temper had been no more than a piece of play-acting, to gain her own ends. Women did that sort of thing.

Wiping her eyes she said: 'So you'll write that story the way I want it written, won't you?'

He capitulated. 'Very well.'

'And let me read it through?'

'Can you read?'

She pretended to be affronted. 'Certainly I can read. I was learned to read before ever I came to London. After a fashion. Anyhow I can read good enough.'

'Very well,' he agreed again. 'You shall read it through.'

'And when it's in print,' she insisted, 'I shall want to read it again, to make sure it's the same. You might have slipped in something that I didn't like.'

He agreed to that too. 'The *Police News* has pictures,' he said. 'Will you come to London with me tomorrow to let an artist make some sketches of you? If you are going to object to that, there will be no point in going on with the story at all.'

'Oh, I don't object to that.' Her vanity was excited. 'Fancy my picture in a printed paper!'

'That's all right then. Can we make another start with the story?'

There and then they made a fresh start, and the work continued during the day. When it was finished and he had put the material together and made a fair copy, he shook his head over it. The thing was too mild altogether. The artist's drawings would sell it. But the reading matter was tame.

Kitty approved of it, however. Handing back the manuscript to him with a pretty air of pride and satisfaction, she said: 'We done that very nicely, I think.'

It was rushed through before the Cassilis Street case had faded from the public mind, but it only sold moderately. The proprietor of the *Illustrated Police News* asked Frank Unwin what he meant by dishing up such milk-and-watery stuff, but neither of them was seriously perturbed. They both knew that there was no end to the supply of murder cases and that the next one might well provide a far more gruesome and libellous and profitable story.

Kitty was delighted with the artist's drawings. But when Frank Unwin offered her the balance of the fifteen pounds he had promised her she refused it.

'No,' she said. 'I didn't do what you wanted. Not really I didn't. So I'm not entitled to the money. And anyhow I've been living here, haven't I? Free board and lodging and everything found . . . But I tell you what. You give me five bob a week for keeping house and looking after your mother. How about that? Until you find someone that suits you better, I mean.'

'Ten bob.'

'Ten bob then. Some folks have got more money than sense.'

Her exasperated tone did not deceive him. She liked living with him and Ma. She was going to stay.

4

Six months later Kitty was still there.

Ma seemed to be failing, but this was no longer a source of worry to her son. Kitty did what was necessary, leaving Frank Unwin to get on with his work.

One day when he was sitting by Ma's bedside, she said: 'Look here, Frank, I can't last more than a year or two at the outside.'

He told her not to be silly. She had many years left if she took things easily.

'I do take things easily. You know that. I used not to but I do now because we've got Kitty. All the same, I don't reckon you'll be bothered with me for much more than a twelvemonth . . . Now what I wanted to say was that you ought to be thinking about what's going to happen to you when I'm not here.'

'Kitty will stay on and keep house for me, I hope.'

She shook her head decisively. 'When I'm gone, you two couldn't live here together without you got married. It wouldn't be decent.'

'Suppose I don't want to get married?'

'Quite time you did. And you might look farther and fare worse than Kitty.'

'Kitty might not accept me.'

'Kitty'd accept you all right. You ask her and see. . . . And another thing, Frank. I'd like to hold a grandchild in my arms before I die. I never had a grandchild, and if you don't look sharp I never shall.' She shifted her position carefully in the bed. 'What you looking so glum about anyhow?' she demanded. 'Kitty's a good-looking woman, a woman that any man ought to be glad to marry. She's been a flighty one, I don't doubt, but she's ready to settle down now. I'm as sure of that as I am that I'm lying here in this bed. Now go and ask her right away like a good boy, and come back and tell me what she says.'

He went off, but not to propose to Kitty. He didn't intend to let Ma or anyone else shove him into Kitty's arms.

Kitty had settled down at Camberwell like a bird on her nest. He had given it out that she was someone that the doctor had recommended to keep house and look after Ma. And the neighbours had never by any word or sign intimated that they recognised her as the woman in the Cassilis Street case. Perhaps none of them read the *Illustrated Police News*. Or if they did, it had not occurred to them that the new arrival at Mrs. Unwin's had anything to do with the picture in the paper. In any case London is not like a country town. It is well known that you can live in a London street for years and remain anonymous.

But if the neighbours didn't know or didn't care, Frank Unwin knew and couldn't help caring. It upset him to think that Kitty had been flighty with men, had been in prison for theft and had come within hailing distance of the hangman. He was upset because he had been growing more and more fond of Kitty. He hated the thought of her past. But he had come to hate still more the thought of his own future without her to share it.

She gave him Irish stew for dinner that day, followed by a rice pudding. Although she had never been in service as a cook, her plain cooking was just what plain cooking should be. The Irish stew was tasty, the rice pudding creamy. They ate the meal together, as they generally did when he was at home, chatting in a desultory way like husband and wife.

When dinner was over he said: 'That was very nice, Kitty.'

'Glad you liked it, I'm sure.'

These small domestic remarks satisfied him, as her plain cooking satisfied him. His eyes rested on her across the table and he was conscious of the stirrings of desire. He had been aware of these stirrings before and had resisted them, thinking of John Berridge and other men. But Ma had said that he ought to marry. Ma wanted to cuddle her grandchild before she died. And it was Kitty that Ma had picked for a daughter-in-law.

Kitty got up and began to clear the table. Then she went upstairs to fetch Ma's tray.

Sitting there with his elbow on the table and his chin cupped in his palm, he came to a decision. It was a sensible decision and he knew that he had been moving towards it of his own accord for some time. Nobody was pushing him. He would do what Ma wanted, but not to please Ma. He would do it because he wanted to do it.

When Kitty returned with the tray he sat back and said: 'How about going to Kew Gardens tomorrow?'

She put the tray down. 'What, you and me, d'you mean?'

'That's right.'

'What about leaving Ma?'

'Ma doesn't mind being left, once in a while. She'd probably be dozing most of the time.'

Kitty hesitated. 'Well, if you think Ma wouldn't mind——'

'I know she wouldn't. About time you had a bit of a spree. It's dull for you here.'

'I don't find it dull. I've been happy here. But I'd like to go to Kew. It would be stunning if the weather was good. Does it cost a lot?'

'Admission free,' he said.

'How should we go? I've never been before.'

'Bus to London Bridge. And then I thought it would be nice to go on the steamboat. There are boats that leave London Bridge every ten minutes or so. You go to Chelsea on one of those and when you reach Chelsea you change on to a steamboat that takes you from the Cadogan Pier there right up the river to Kew Gardens. I know, because I've been myself.'

'You have, have you? And who did you take with you, may I enquire?'

The little flash of jealousy did not displease him. 'I took my Aunt Harriet,' he said.

She went over to the window and looked up at the cloudless sky. 'It'll be lovely if it's like this.'

'We must take some sandwiches.'

'I'll see to that.'

She did see to it, as she saw to everything. And the trip to Kew proved a great success. The weather was perfect, the boats comfortable, the sandwiches delicious. In a quiet corner of Kew Gardens he proposed to her.

'Oh, look here, this is taking me by surprise.' She affected dismay. 'I'm quite happy as I am.'

'Think it over,' he said, 'and then tell me. You're old enough to know your own mind.'

'I'm not all that old,' she protested. 'How long will you give me to make my mind up?'

'Ten minutes.'

She sighed. 'The trouble is I take a fancy to men,' she said. 'I can't trust myself really. I been all right these last six months with you and Ma. But I might break out again. And what would you do then, if you were married to me?'

'Give you the hiding of your life,' he told her.

She looked down at his little figure and laughed out loud, throwing back her head.

'I can just see you doing it,' she said.

'I earn about two hundred pounds a year,' he went on, 'taking one week with another. That's enough to live on. Just Ma and us and a baby.'

'Mr. Unwin, I like that, I do really. Baby indeed. Better learn to walk before you run, hadn't you?'

He did not insist on the ten minutes' time limit. But when they got back to Camberwell they were engaged to be married.

She wasn't in love with him. He had never supposed that she might be. But she was fond of him and used to him. At his age, and perhaps at hers too, that wasn't a bad basis for marriage.

Her love, he suspected, had been given to young Stephen Berridge, who hadn't wanted it. She had no more love of that sort to give. But she still had fondness and affection to bestow, and the warm sunshine of her vitality.

Six weeks later, to the day, she was Mrs. Unwin. Frank Unwin, as they left the church together, felt foolishly proud of her.

8

I

RUTH BERRIDGE had taken it for granted for most of her life that she was a bookish girl, interested chiefly in poetry and novels, the improving lectures that she sometimes went to, and the contents of museums and art galleries. Of men and marriage she had hardly thought at all. When she glanced rather timidly at the future, she saw herself becoming a contented spinster. She had known such women and it had not seemed to her that they were less happy than their married sisters.

This attitude of mind lasted until the day when the boy Baxter discovered that horrid thing in the cellar. Looking back, indeed, Ruth suspected that a change had already been taking place before this. From the time of Stephen's disappearance, perhaps, or even earlier. She found herself glancing at men with a speculative eye now, wondering what they would be like as husbands. And she paid more attention to her appearance. As a result, men took more notice of her, and she enjoyed this. Being a woman, she perceived, could be quite exciting.

The lease of the house in Cassilis Street ended several weeks after the trial of Kitty Daniels. Ruth had heard her parents talking about whether they would renew the lease. Eventually, she was told, the landlord had agreed to let Dad continue in the house on a quarterly tenancy. The future was uncertain, but for the moment Lizzie Siddle kept the lodging-house running smoothly.

Mother put the trial unobtrusively behind her and never mentioned it, but it seemed to have aged Dad. He was no longer the well-preserved man that he had been. His hair was quite grey now and his fine eyes lacked their former lustre. The domestic atmosphere at Cassilis Street was depressing.

Over at Windsor Aunt Sophy died suddenly, leaving Mother very much more money than Mother, with her modest ideas, had ever expected. Dad hinted at retirement.

Stephen's whereabouts remained a matter of mystery and conjecture. Mother stuck to her theory of the debt of honour, and Dad said nothing.

Nor was anything heard of the fate of Kitty Daniels. After the trial, she seemed to vanish as completely as Stephen had done. Not even Nelly Cloke knew what had happened to her. Dad's friend Mr. Sainsbury reported that a story supposed to have been written by Kitty had appeared in the *Illustrated Police News.*

'It is not likely that she wrote it herself,' Mr. Sainsbury said. 'Some Grub-street hack's work, I don't doubt. It isn't the kind of journal that we should have at home, but I happened to see a copy at the office.'

The Sainsburys were in the private parlour at Cassilis Street. They were loyal friends, whom scandal did not keep away.

'The article about Kitty Daniels was surprisingly mild,' Mr. Sainsbury went on, 'considering the sort of paper it appeared in. And there was a recognisable picture of the lady herself. Quite a good likeness, it was.'

'Whether it was a good likeness or not is of no importance,' said Mrs. Sainsbury heavily. 'The whole thing is over and done with, and that is what matters. The less said about it, the better.'

Ruth, feeling a little sorry for Mr. Sainsbury, asked him where he and Mrs. Sainsbury were going for their summer holiday.

'I am hard up.' Mr. Sainsbury, not at all put out by his wife's censorious remarks, made a comical face and pretended to turn out his pockets. 'I can't afford summer holidays.'

'Don't take any notice of him, Ruth,' said Mrs. Sainsbury. 'He has quite enough money for a holiday and we are going to Weston-super-Mare. It is all arranged.'

Mother mentioned a young couple she knew, who had gone to Weston-super-Mare for their honeymoon and found the place very bracing.

'When you're on your honeymoon, any place is delightful.' Mr. Sainsbury winked daringly at Ruth. 'When are you going to have a honeymoon, Ruth?'

Mrs. Sainsbury pursed her lips. 'That is quite enough,' she told her husband.

Ruth simpered, as she was expected to do, and Mrs. Sainsbury began to talk about her daughter Agnes, who had become engaged recently to her cousin. It would probably have to be a long engagement. But at least they knew all about the young man.

Ruth didn't envy Agnes Sainsbury. Marrying your cousin wasn't very romantic. She herself, twice during the last month, had seen a most interesting young man in the National Gallery, where she sometimes went to look at the pictures. On the second occasion he bowed and half-smiled but did not speak. Obviously he was intellectual and artistic, or he would not have been there, twice in a month. In her mind, as she did not know his name, she called him Mr. X. She felt sure that Fate must have thrown them together. Also, more prosaically, she wondered whether he was in a position to marry.

2

Ruth thought no more about the *Illustrated Police News* until, one evening not long after the Sainsburys' visit, a woman called at Cassilis Street with a copy of the paper in question in her hand. Mother and Dad were out. Since the trial, Dad had been asked to resign his chapel membership, because of the disclosures about his behaviour with Kitty. Mother had resigned too but she sometimes attended another chapel with Ruth. Dad never went to any place of worship now.

On this particular evening, therefore, instead of being at a chapel meeting, Mother and Dad had gone to hear Christy's Minstrels at the concert-room attached to Her Majesty's Theatre, Mother being so particularly fond of the Christy Minstrel songs. Ruth did not go with them. Dad had asked her in a half-hearted way whether she would like to come, but she suspected that he and Mother did not really want her. So she was at home reading a novel when the front-door bell rang and Lizzie came to tell her that there was a woman at the door enquiring for Master.

'He is out,' Ruth said, 'and Mother too. They won't be coming home until quite late.'

'I know they are out, miss. Missus told me they were going. The person wanted to know if she could see you, as there was nobody else at home belonging to the family.'

Ruth was annoyed at being dragged away from the romantic world of her novel.

'Didn't she say what she wanted, Lizzie?'

'No, miss.'

'Very well. I will come out in a minute or two.'

She read on to the bottom of the page, then went out to the entrance hall. The woman, small, elderly and quite well dressed, was seated nervously on the edge of a chair and clutching what looked like a newspaper of some kind.

'Miss Berridge?' she said, standing up and peering at Ruth through spectacles.

'Yes, I am Miss Berridge. Can I help you?'

'It was Mr. Berridge I really wanted to see. Or Mrs. Berridge. But as they are out, perhaps you can tell me what I ought to do. I don't want to get into any trouble, you see. I only want to do what's right.'

'Could you call and see my father at his shop in Tottenham Court Road?' Ruth suggested. 'He will be there tomorrow morning.'

'No good, miss. I'm only in London for a few hours. I live in the country now, see, out at Barnet, and I've got to get back tonight, because of my sister being alone.' She thrust towards Ruth the crumpled journal that she had been carrying. 'It's this, miss. The *Police News*. This is the house where the murder was committed, isn't it?'

Ruth took the paper with distaste. It was open at a page that bore the headline: *The Horrible Cassilis Street Case*. And she could see, among other drawings, the recognisable likeness of Kitty that Mr. Sainsbury had been talking about.

'Is that the servant that used to work here?' asked the visitor.

'I think it is supposed to be.'

'The one who got off at the trial?'

'Yes.'

'She was guilty,' said the little woman decisively, 'and I tell you for why.'

Ruth was horrified, but she could not dam the spate of words. It appeared that the woman was called Carey, Mrs. Carey. She lived with her sister at Barnet now, her sister being in poor health. They were both widows. Until a year ago, when her sister's husband died, Mrs. Carey had been in business at King's Cross as a dealer in second-hand clothes.

'Then when my brother-in-law died and my sister was so

queer, I decided to close the shop and go and live with my sister, which I did.'

Ruth tried again to stop her. 'What has all this to do with me, Mrs. Carey?'

'I'll tell you, my dear. It was this paper, see? I never took it in but my sister does and I look at it sometimes. And happening to see that picture, I recognised the person.' She allowed herself a dramatic pause. 'I recognised her at once as a woman who came five or six times to my shop about two years ago. This woman brought me silk dresses and lace petticoats, that she said had been left her by a relation that had died, but as she didn't care to wear a dead person's clothes she was selling them. I bought the stuff off her and paid her a good price. She gave a name but I forget what it was. And an address too. It was all lies anyway, I can see that now.'

At this moment Mr. Walker came in at the front door. The brusque young Lancashire man who had been the first lodger was still brusque, though not quite as young. Living in London for three years had wrought some changes in him but they were mostly superficial. He raised his hat as he passed Ruth and said: 'Good-evening, Miss Berridge.'

When he had gone up the stairs the little woman came back to her main point.

'Now what I want to know, dear, is this. What ought I to do?'

'You must really wait until you can see my father, Mrs. Carey.'

'No, miss. I want to get it settled tonight. It's on my mind, see. When that skeleton was found in your cellar, I don't doubt the police went to all the secon-hand-clothes shops in London. They are thorough, the police are. They come to me pretty often when I had my shop, and I tells them whatever I knows. Fair's fair, isn't it, miss? I never had anything to do with shielding criminals and never will. But by the time the police had found that skeleton and started their enquiry, my shop was closed, more's the pity. . . . Now, miss, what ought I to do?'

Ruth tried to wriggle away from the question. 'It seems to me that you are short-sighted, Mrs. Carey, if you will forgive my mentioning it. Might you not be mistaken in thinking that you recognised the picture of Kitty Daniels as the woman who called on you two years ago? After all, it is a long time. And you only saw her a few times.'

It was useless. 'I made no mistake, miss. As soon as I saw that paper I said to my sister, "That's the woman that sold me those silk dresses and petticoats". At once I said it. Without hesitation. In my opinion those dresses and petticoats had belonged to the poor lady that was murdered. And if this Kitty Daniels hadn't done the murder, what was she doing with the lady's clothes?'

The little woman sat down again. She was not going to leave until she had got a straight answer. Ruth, searching desperately in her mind for a source from which she might expect help, thought of a plan.

'Wait here for two minutes, Mrs. Carey,' she said. 'I will try to find a gentleman who may be able to assist you.'

'What gentleman's that?' asked Mrs. Carey suspiciously.

'A friend of the family who lives here.'

'Very well, dear. I'll wait.'

Ruth hurried up to Mr. Walker's room. She had hardly ever been inside his room, for she had practically nothing to do with the lodgers, and what she had seen of Mr. Walker had not made her wish to know him better. But he had been in the house longer than any of the other lodgers, and though he was not strictly a friend of the family, he was the nearest thing to it available at short notice just then.

At his door she paused to collect her ideas and pat her hair. Then she knocked.

Mr. Walker opened the door smartly. He had taken off his coat and his feet were in slippers.

'I am sorry to disturb you, Mr. Walker. I wonder whether you can advise me.'

'Pleased to help you if I can. What's up?'

'That woman you saw me talking to in the hall has come about Kitty—Kitty Daniels that used to be here.' Earnestly and hopefully, she repeated as much as she could remember of what the second-hand-clothes dealer had said. 'What am I to tell her?' she pleaded finally.

He smiled in a masculine, protective sort of way. 'I'll tell her all she needs to know,' he said. 'Wait till I get my coat on again.'

She stood at the door while he fetched his coat. He had not invited her to cross his threshold and she approved of this. It showed caution and good sense. And it did not escape her that his room looked as if he was orderly in his habits, which was another good thing in a man.

They went down to the hall together and Ruth said: 'This is Mr. Walker, the friend that I mentioned to you. I am sure he will be able to help you.'

'Hope so in case not.' The woman got up from her chair. 'Though I don't know as it's help I want. A plain answer would be enough. Has the young lady told you what I want to know, sir?'

'She has. And the plain answer is that it's no good coming here. If you wish to make a disclosure, you must go to the police. Do you know where the nearest police station is?'

'Yes, sir.' Mr. Walker's authoritative manner was producing the right effect. 'I used to have a shop at King's Cross, see. So I know the district.'

'Very well then. Go to the police if you wish. But of course, nothing that you say now will alter the verdict at the recent trial. You are too late to give evidence. The trial is over and the verdict of Not Guilty cannot be upset.'

The woman blinked at him. 'How am I to know that what

you say is right, sir?' she ventured. 'I want to be sure, you do understand that, sir, don't you?'

'If you don't believe me, go to the police.'

'But you think I'll be wasting my time. You think I might as well keep my mouth shut. That's what you think, is it?'

'What I think is neither here nor there. You must do what you like about going to the police. But it's no use coming to Mr. Berridge.'

She looked from Mr. Walker to Ruth and back again, then she gave it up. 'I may as well be going,' she muttered. Ruth opened the front door for her and watched her as she went cautiously down the front steps.

Mr. Walker was still standing in the hall. He was grinning amiably and something about him suggested that, after seeing her casually for three years, he had just realised that she was an attractive young woman.

'I reckon we shan't hear any more of that old party,' he said.

'Thank you so much for talking to her. I can't tell you how grateful I am.'

'You don't need to be grateful. It was easy enough.'

'Easy for you, Mr. Walker.'

'Are you going to tell your parents?'

'Do you think I ought to?'

'Who am I to say what a young lady ought to do, Miss Berridge? But in your shoes I should say nowt and take a chance on the short-sighted old party going straight home and putting the whole matter out of her mind. You don't want to worry your parents. They've had enough worry, one way and another. And whatever the old girl does makes no difference. Kitty got off and that's that.'

She gazed up at him admiringly. Here, in her own home, was a man to depend on. And a man to dally with too, which wasn't to be disregarded. It was like finding gold in the back-yard.

They dallied agreeably at the foot of the stairs for a little longer. Then she went back to her novel. But it no longer held her attention. Her mind kept drifting off to the short-sighted woman, whom Mr. Walker had disposed of in such a manly, resolute fashion. She wondered what his Christian name was and whether he was engaged to some young woman whom he had known in Lancashire.

Shadowy, artistic Mr. X in the National Gallery was relegated to the dim background of her thoughts. Mr. X, she felt sure, would never have dealt with the second-hand-clothes dealer as capably as Mr. Walker had done.

A week later, with Mother's permission, he took Ruth to the Crystal Palace.

3

Mr. Walker's Christian name proved to be Alfred. And there was no young woman in Lancashire.

By the end of June he had proposed, and Ruth had accepted him. He was not a novelist's hero like Mr. X but she knew that she would always be safe with him. Mother and Dad seemed pleased. For the moment at least, they didn't need her. Later on, if one of them died, the other might turn to her. She hoped that she would be a good daughter, whatever happened. But she had never envied the lot of those unwedded daughters who lived on, year after year, in a widowed parent's home, playing the thankless rôle of the companion-housekeeper who could never give notice.

Alfred satisfied Dad that he was in a position to support a wife and the arrangements for the marriage went slowly forward. Ruth was in no hurry. She wanted to enjoy the sensation of being engaged, before it was lost in the more challenging delights of marriage. She had convinced herself that she was in love with Alfred. And she knew that he was certainly in love with her.

It was a winter wedding but the day was as mild as spring. The honeymoon was spent at Torquay, and afterwards they went home, not to Cassilis Street or anywhere else in that part of London, but to a house that Alfred had rented in Camberwell. He had thought it advisable that they should live a fair distance away from Ruth's parents. And Camberwell suited him from a business point of view as he could get to and from the City easily. The house was not, however, at the Walworth Road end of Camberwell but further south, in select Brunswick Square. It was semi-detached, not a terrace house, and it contained a large dining-room and a slightly smaller drawing-room, a breakfast-room and seven bedrooms. Also the tenancy conferred the right to use the gardens around which the houses in the square were built. The rent was seventy pounds a year, which seemed a lot of money to Ruth, but she accepted Alfred's statement that the house was well worth it.

'It's far and away the best address in Camberwell,' he told her. 'We shan't want all the bedrooms, of course. Not yet awhile, any road. But it's a fine house to invite business people do. When they see that house, they can be sure that Alf Walker is going up the ladder reet fast. It's good for a man's business reputation to have a house like that.'

Alfred was all for business. She didn't know how much money he had, but he wasn't a mean man.

Most of the time she was quite happy with him. He could be boring or irritating sometimes, but not often. And he was reliable. He would always stand by her, as he had done in the entrance-hall at Cassilis Street, when she had gone to him for help.

Nothing more, so far as she knew, had ever been heard about the short-sighted second-hand-clothes woman.

Alfred need not have worried about living too near his wife's parents, because Dad gave up the tenancy of the Cassilis Street house on the Ladyday following the wedding, and sold his furniture business soon after. Mother and Dad went to live at Windsor in Aunt Sophy's old house. It had been left to her in Aunt Sophy's will and she had refused to sell it, thinking that one day she might be able to live there herself.

Ruth was glad that the connection with Cassilis Street had been broken. There was always a dark stain on the association, and the house was never by any chance mentioned when Alfred's business friends came to Brunswick Square to dine. Nor was the trial of Kitty Daniels ever referred to. Kitty Daniels herself, once so much the life and soul of the house at Cassilis Street, belonged to the past in the same way that poor Stephen did. Ruth always called him poor Stephen when she spoke of him at all.

'I don't know why he has got to be poor Stephen,' Alfred said once. 'It's my belief that your brother isn't short of brass. Better off than we are, lass, I'll be bound. Though he doesn't have to work hard for his money like your hubby, I'll bet a shilling.'

Alfred was not a betting man. Even when he was merely emphasising an opinion, his verbal bets did not exceed a shilling.

He had never liked Stephen, it seemed. But he conceded that, in his view, Stephen had somehow or other been sharp enough to feather his nest very comfortably indeed.

Whether this was true or not, Stephen never reappeared on the stage of Ruth's life. But, one day in Camberwell, Kitty Daniels did.

It was an October morning. Ruth was out shopping when she met Kitty face to face. Kitty was pushing a bassinet.

'Well, Miss Ruth!' Kitty's smile, as of old, was like sunshine. 'Fancy meeting you, miss!'

It was difficult to be stand-offish with Kitty. Ruth said: 'You look very well and happy, I must say, Kitty. Have you a situation in Camberwell now?'

Kitty laughed, throwing back her head. 'In a manner of speaking I suppose you might say I have, miss. I am married, you see, and I have my husband to look after and his old mother who's bedridden and this baby.'

Ruth bent over the bassinet, took off her left glove and stroked the baby's soft cheek. The baby smiled up at her. There was no need to ask who the mother was, for the smile was the image of Kitty's.

'A little girl, is it?' she said.

'Yes, a little girl. Little Minnie.'

'Is she called after somebody in the family?'

'No. We just liked the name, both of us. And it didn't go too badly with the surname, which is Unwin. Frank Unwin my husband's name is. I've been Mrs. Unwin for the last fifteen months.'

'How old is Minnie?' Ruth asked.

'Nearly three months now.'

'You live near here, do you, Kitty?'

'Yes.' She mentioned the street. 'But you don't live round here, do you, Miss Ruth?'

'Yes, I do now. In Brunswick Square, Camberwell.'

'Brunswick Square, Camberwell? Oh yes, I know. Very nice indeed. I used to work in Brunswick Square in London once, as you may remember. Quite a coincidence when you come to think of it.' She paused delicately. 'Your parents are both well, I hope?'

'Quite well. They have moved to Windsor.'

'Have they really? Well, fancy that . . . So you're married now, are you, Miss Ruth?'

'Yes.' The wedding ring naturally hadn't escaped Kitty's attention. 'I am Mrs. Walker. Do you recollect Mr. Walker at Cassilis Street?'

Kitty's mouth opened and closed again, and the expression of surprise on her face changed to one of congratulation.

'Well, that is a bit of news, miss,' she said. 'A very capable young man I always thought, if you will pardon the liberty. A hard worker, I should say. Had his head screwed on right, Mr. Walker did. When were you married, miss?'

'In January.'

'Well, I hope you'll be very happy. I do indeed.'

'You too, Kitty.'

'Thank you, miss.'

Ruth leaned over the bassinet again, making baby-talk noises, while they discussed Minnie's weight and clothing and nocturnal habits. Ruth was in an interesting condition herself, and babies were in the forefront of her mind.

'Does she cry much in the day-time?' she asked Kitty.

'Not much. She's got an obliging disposition, I reckon.'

They talked about Minnie for a little longer, then Ruth said: 'We shall be meeting again one day, Kitty, I expect.'

'I hope so, I'm sure You'll give my regards to Mr. Walker, won't you, miss?'

Ruth promised to do so and they said good-bye. She kept her promise that evening, and Alfred said it sounded as though Kitty had fallen on her feet.

'Did she ask after poor Stephen?' he enquired with a grin.

'No. She didn't mention him.'

He grunted, as though there were comments in his mind which he thought it wiser to keep to himself.

'What did you talk about?' he asked.

'About the baby mostly.'

'Always a safe topic with the ladies, eh?' He patted her knee fondly. It was not many weeks ago that she had told him that he was to be a father. 'Kitty Daniels,' he added, 'was a remarkable woman. Too good for a housemaid.'

He spoke as if she had died. But of course Kitty hadn't died. She had merely settled down. They had all settled down. Ruth herself, and Mother and Dad, even perhaps poor Stephen. And the house in Cassilis Street where that dreadful thing had happened, no doubt that had settled down too, with new tenants and different lodgers.

Afred began to tell her about a profitable stroke of business that he had pulled off that day. It was an exciting story for him to tell, but dull for her to listen to. Nevertheless she listened dutifully, making appropriate little remarks, while she thought about Kitty and Kitty's baby, and wondered whether she herself would have a boy or a girl.